HER DIRTY MECHANICS

MIKA LANE

HEADLANDS PUBLISHING

BE THE FIRST TO KNOW...

Want more heat, heart,
and bad boys who know what they're doing?
Join my list and I'll send the steam straight to your inbox,
starting with a deliciously naughty story:

SIGN UP TO MY MAILING LIST!
Or visit:
https://geni.us/free-book-signup

NELLA BRYSON

Happy fucking birthday.

To me.

There was nothing like waking up on one's special day to the sound of roommates, total strangers a mere month ago, getting it on in the shower.

Loudly.

Actually, very loudly, no to mention, right next door to my bedroom. The shower shared a wall with the head of my Ikea bed frame.

Which was not the sturdiest thing in the world. As my roommates drilled each other against the shower tile, their enthusiasm bounced through to wall, shaking my bed in the process.

"Tommy," my roommate screamed, "fill me with your hot cum. Do it, baby!"

I so did not need this.

I could have used another half hour of sleep before my shift at Mug Me Coffee, but there was no hope of that now. I was awake. Wide awake. And hoping the thin wall separating me from my roommates' fucking was going to remain standing.

Not that this was their first time… enjoying each other… whether in the shower or anywhere else in the house.

Like the kitchen. Or the living room.

I'd even come across them in the foyer.

But when they chose the bathroom to celebrate their great fortune in finding each other, I wondered how long it would take to burst through the wall into my room—wet, soapy, in the throes of multiple orgasms, the likes of which I'd only ever been able to give myself.

But that was another problem for another day.

The most pressing issue, now that I was up, was where I was supposed to get ready for work. My roommates and I—the three of us—shared one bathroom. And from the sound of it, I was not going to get in there anytime soon.

Because I'd been through this before, I grabbed my toothbrush and hustled down to the kitchen sink, full of dirty dishes from the night before, and started washing up. I'd have to wait to pee till I got to work.

But that was life in New York for a barista like me. I didn't earn enough at Mug Me to live alone, and even sharing an apartment here in the Big Apple, I still had to sacrifice the usual amenities—like a private bathroom.

People like me did not have private bathrooms. They shared them with two other roommates, or any of the general public that decided it wanted to use the Mug Me rest room. Those were the two bathrooms in my life.

But it was all good. Minor discomforts aside, I liked my life in New York.

And I didn't mind that my roommates had hooked up. I just wished they were quieter about their… enthusiasm.

I pulled on my sneakers, black jeans, and white T-shirt—the barista uniform of Mug Me—and set out for work at a fast clip.

I really had to pee.

"Look who it is," my coworker Jelly cried when I burst in the front door, dashing past her for the ladies room.

"Birthday girl!" she yelled to the rest of the team

Some birthday.

"Be right back," I called to the crew, leaving behind a chorus of *happy birthdays*.

"Roommates fucking again?" Jelly yelled after me.

Funny thing about New York was that you could shout something like that out in a coffee shop and no one batted an eye.

No one gave a shit what you did, as long as you didn't bother them. It was such a far cry from the small town I'd grown up in—and couldn't wait to get the hell out of—where everybody knew your business before you even did.

A quick minute later, I joined my coworkers for the morning rush, tying on my black barista apron, followed by a hairband since my hair was too short for a ponytail.

When I'd started, the manager had no idea what to do with a woman whose hair was too short for a ponytail. He'd actually had the nerve to look at my black, swingy bob—which I liked very much—with disdain, as if I'd styled my hair this way on purpose to fuck with him and his stupid rules about hair and ponytail-wearing.

The morning was flying by, and after some guy ordered a ten-step coffee drink and left without tipping even a nickel, it was time for my break. The morning had been crazy, with lines out the door, but I couldn't complain. Busy was good. Made the time go by faster, and meant that my employment was secure.

And when I arrived in the breakroom, Jelly was there with a birthday candle in a strawberry scone—my favorite pastry in all the coffee shop.

"Happy birthday, Nella," she beamed, holding the scone so I could make a wish and blow.

She was such a good friend.

"How's your birthday going so far?" she asked, helping herself to a corner of it after I'd blown out my candle.

I didn't mind sharing. Not with Jelly. She was my ride or die.

I popped another corner of scone into my mouth. "It's good, thanks. Nothing big to report. Mmmm. Good scone."

She sidled up next to me at the sticky breakroom table. "Want to hit up Mixer's tonight? They have two-dollar gin and tonics from six to seven."

Mixer's was our place. In fact, it was the place for everyone in New York who either couldn't afford full-price drinks, or didn't want to. Jelly and I would speed drink, and consume whatever they had on special from six to seven p.m., and then nurse one drink for the next few hours while we hung out.

But tonight was not a Mixer's night.

"I'm actually working a double shift—"

"On your birthday?" she interrupted, horror crisscrossing her face.

"Yeah. I'm saving up to see if maybe I can get my own place at some point."

She looked at me like that was even crazier than working on my birthday. "Get your own place? Like here, in Manhattan?"

"Jelly, it's not like it's never been done…" I trailed off because she had a point. People like us didn't have *our own places.*

"Well, I'm saving for something, then. If not my own apartment, then… whatever."

There was a muffled sound behind us. We turned in the direction of a buzzing phone, stuffed into the pocket of one of the many jackets hanging on the breakroom wall.

"That phone has been buzzing all morning. Wonder whose it is," she said.

Shit. Was that coming the direction of *my* hoodie?

I got up and pulled it out of my pocket. "Wow. Six calls from my brother. Probably to wish me happy birthday."

I started to put my phone back, when it buzzed again.

And when I thought about it, my brother would never call me six times on my birthday, or any other day.

What was going on?

Jelly scarfed the last of my scone crumbs and skipped back to work, while I dialed my brother.

"Robert Bryson's office. How may I help you?" a very officious admin answered.

"Hey, Charlotte," I said, mainly because I knew she hated when I acted all familiar with her, "it's me, Nella, calling for Robbie."

She clucked her tongue, no doubt for a variety of reasons, and finished expressing how insulted she was with a loud sigh.

"Mr. Bryson is not available—"

"Charlotte, he's already called me six times today. I really need to speak with him."

She harrumphed, mumbled something, then patched me through.

"Robert Bryson," my brother said in an extra-deep voice.

It was interesting. Ever since he'd started working for a New York law firm, his voice had mysteriously deepened.

"Hey, Robbie, it's me. That admin of yours is a piece of work—"

"Nella, my name is *Robert* now. Not *Robbie*."

Another thing about his New York arrival. His lifelong nickname, Robbie, had been put to rest, replaced by his given name. But old habits died hard. I didn't think I'd ever call him Robert. And that irritated the shit out of him.

His admin too, it seemed.

"Sorry. I keep forgetting," I said, waiting for him to wish me happy birthday and offer to take me out to a nice dinner.

The only time I had nice dinners these days was when Robbie—I mean, Robert—was in the mood to treat his little sister. Which wasn't very often.

Yeah, we'd both left our small town, but sometimes I felt like Robbie wished he could leave me, too. He was On His Way Up, as he liked to remind me, and had to hang out with like-minded people.

Not his loser barista sister.

"Hey, Robbie, you know today is my—"

"Look, Nella, I only have a minute. You need to go home."

"Home? Why? I can't go home until after my shift ends."

"No. *Home-home.* Like our real home. Well, *your* home, anyway."

"Do you mean Dad's home? Like where we grew up, home? Hey, it's just as much yours as mine. And why do I have to go there, anyway?"

I looked at the big Mug Me clock on the wall. Break time was almost up, and I didn't have time to keep arguing with my brother.

"Robbie, what is going on?"

"It's Dad."

2

NELLA BRYSON

I SHIFTED MY BUNCHED-UP HOODIE AGAINST THE BUS window to use as a pillow, but it was of no use. Sleep didn't seem in the cards for me.

Which sucked because it was one a.m. and I was dead tired. But such is life when you take the cheap bus out of New York. Want to save some money and travel five hundred miles for twenty dollars? You're going to have to do it in the middle of the night on a bus packed to the gills, which smelled like a combination of beef jerky and Chinese food. Oh, and someone in the back might be smoking a joint.

At least it wasn't a cigarette.

And since I was wide awake, I kept playing the conversation I'd had with my brother, over and over.

Because he was five years older, we'd never really hung out much, so we weren't particularly close. After a disastrous first semester at college, when he'd been sent home with his tail between his legs, he'd quickly gotten his shit together and never looked back. Since that time, he'd been nose-down, determined to become another New York master of the universe—as if they didn't already have enough.

So, it didn't come as a surprise that he expected me to drop everything and head back to the town where we'd grown up to help my dad, who'd taken a tumble off a ladder cleaning gutters and busted the crap out of one of his legs.

Of course, I wanted to help my father. But the way Robbie went about demanding that I be the one to head home instead of him, was going to rub me the wrong way for a long time to come.

Yeah, he was my brother and all, but he was still pretty much of a douchebag.

I told him I couldn't just leave at the drop of a hat. "Robbie, I have a job. And I'm on the schedule all week, with some double shifts. Like the one I'm working today. Which, by the way, is my birthday. Why can't you go home to help dad? You want me to get fired?"

He sighed, just like his admin had. "First, Nella," he said with forced calm, "I can't just pick up and leave. You might not know this, but I was recently made partner here. I have a lot on my shoulders and couldn't possibly let the firm down. Second, they can't fire you for leaving to help a sick family member. And if they do, I'll sue their asses. I'm an attorney, remember? And last, I haven't been back there in three years. Dad's probably pissed at me. So, it's better that you go."

Good thing he reminded me he was an attorney. Like I could ever forget. He was so proud of himself I was sure everyone in a ten-block radius of his life knew he was.

And now a partner, too, I guess.

I decided to dig my heels in. "Well, if you won't go, I won't go. I'm taking on extra work so I can get my own apartment. I'm very busy, myself."

He chuckled. Yeah, he was the kind of guy who chuckled. "Nella, you'll never get your own apart- ment on what you make as a barista—"

"I've about had it with people who don't support my goals," I interrupted.

He groaned. "Okay. Okay, I'm sorry. But don't you think it's easier for you to go help dad? Nella, you work in a coffee shop. You live with two other roommates in an apartment where you turned the living room into a bedroom to add one more person. Do you even own any furniture?"

Oh no. He did not just say that.

"Robbie, I don't know where you get off thinking your life is so damn important. I have responsibilities and commitments, too."

In the background, a door opened, and a female voice spoke. After several mmm-hmms on Robbie's part, the door closed.

"Nell, I have to get back to work. But hey. Let me pay your way back home."

Why did he keep calling it *home*? It was clearly the last place on earth either of us wanted to be.

"Oooh, so generous of you, Robbie. You can't find time to help out Dad, so you just throw money at the problem. Well, I have my own money and will pay my own way."

"One other thing, Nella."

"What? What else is there?"

"The name is Robert. Not Robbie."

Yeah. Good luck with that.

As the bus stopped in bumfuck nowhere for a truck stop bathroom break, I realized I was trapped in my seat by the person sitting next to me, who was not only sound asleep but also had his head on my shoulder.

I should have accepted Robbie's money.

3

JAKE PARKER

"WON'T YOU TAKE A RIDE WITH ME?"

Well, shit. Mrs. Peters, my old teacher from elementary school, was putting the screws to me. Again. She came in on a regular basis, always with something mysteriously wrong with her car.

Which usually turned out to be not much of anything.

Although she did waste a lot of our time, especially mine. For some reason, she had a thing for me.

Just what I needed, an octogenarian stalker.

"Mrs. Peters, we have several cars ahead of yours. You know we work on them in the order they come in. Now, how fair would it be to repair, say, Doctor Gleason's car first, if yours had come in ahead of his?"

She considered me for a moment, then rejected my logic. "Jake, I have been coming to Bryson's Garage for years, and I expect to be treated like an important customer." Holding her head high, she sniffed.

For fuck's sake. It was the middle of the week, and we were beyond slammed. What sucked about that was if we didn't finish all the cars we had by end of day Friday, we'd have to come in on the weekend.

Not that I didn't want to make overtime. It was just that I was trying to complete a 'suggested reading list' before I started filling out my college applications. As it was, I'd made little progress and was scrambling to catch up.

Mrs. Peters sidled up to me, so close I could see the dark roots beneath her unnaturally bright red hair, and makeup coagulating in the creases under her eyes. Rumor had it that in her younger days, she'd been a beauty queen. But I'd only ever known her as an elementary school teacher—one that everyone in town had at one point or another—and a mean one at that.

After retiring, she married some rich guy who promptly passed away. Since then, she'd waved his money around like it would part the waters of the Red Sea if she demanded it.

And her demands extended to me and the guys here at the garage. To our perpetual dismay, she thought her money entitled her to… well, us. And she usually focused on me, I supposed because I was the youngest of the crew.

Yup. She'd been trying to get in the pants of any of us guys for as long as we could remember. And boy, did she get pissed when we turned her down.

Which meant she was pissed a lot.

Smiling up at me, she pushed her boobs together, her chest turning into a field of wrinkles like my grandmother used to have.

My *teacher*.

"Jake-y, let's go for a little ride, huh? You really have to hear the car's problem. I… just can't really explain it. But it's very frightening. I think it might be about to explode."

She wanted to go for a ride in a car she thought might explode?

I looked back into the garage bay where my coworkers Sebastian and Gus were deep into diagnosing the cars they were working on, and I glanced out to the parking lot to the car I was supposed to have started on a half hour ago.

The weekend was fizzling before my very eyes.

"All right, Mrs. Peters. Let's take a quick ride around the block."

Her face brightened, and she jingled her keys. "Great. Let's go."

I hollered to the guys that I'd be right back, and when they saw me with her, they nodded knowingly. They were happy to dump her on me because that meant they didn't have to deal with her.

Thanks, guys.

"Okay," she said, pulling into traffic without looking, "do you hear that?"

I heard nothing. But I kept listening.

"How about now?" She stopped for a light, and a quiet *thump* sounded from somewhere in the rear of the car.

I nodded quietly, trying to see if it repeated.

"See, I told you. I told you there was something wrong with my car. Oooh! Did you hear that? It just did it again."

I was pretty sure I knew what was up, but instructed Mrs. Peters to return to the garage by making a right turn and then a left, blasting through every *stop* sign we passed. The more she turned the car, the louder the sound got.

When she pulled in, she turned the car off. "What should I do?" she asked, inching closer to me in the passenger seat.

"May I see the keys?" I asked.

She handed them to me. "Do you think you can fix it, Jake? I really don't know what I'll do if you can't."

Time to get the hell out of the car. Mrs. Peters had finished her last sentence by placing a hand on my thigh.

All I could think about was getting the fuck out of the vehicle.

I walked around to the trunk of the car, and opened it. There sat, innocently enough, a can of Campbell's tomato soup. I grabbed it and brought it around to the driver's seat, where Mrs. Peters was fixing her lipstick.

"It was this. Rolling around in your trunk," I said, holding it for her inspection.

She slowly reached for it and took it from me. "Really? Are you sure?" She turned it over in her hands like she'd never seen a can of soup before.

"Mrs. Peters, go drive the car for a bit. See if you hear that sound again."

Sebastian stuck his head out the door. "Jake, we need you in here."

Thank god. I was hoping someone would rescue me.

Mrs. Peter's mouth dropped open. "I... I can't

believe that's all it was. Just a can of… soup." She giggled sheepishly.

"Be right there, Seb," I called. "I think you're good to go now."

She shook her head. "I don't know how I missed that. I mean, I have been really busy, and my dog died on top of that."

I looked back at the office, where the phone was ringing off the hook.

"Gotta run, Mrs. Peters," I said, dashing back inside.

"You mechanics are so good to me," she called after me.

Sebastian and Gus joined me in the office, laughing their asses off.

"Dude, you should have seen your face," Gus said, trying to catch his breath.

Sebastian put an arm around my shoulders. "Did she put her hand on your thigh, and beg you for a riiiiiide?" he asked.

I flipped them off. "Fuck you, guys. You know she was my elementary school teacher. That shit creeps me out. Next time, you can handle her."

Sebastian's face got serious, and he ran his fingers through his long rat's nest of hair. "Speaking of handling women, I have something to discuss with you guys. Could you both take a seat, please?"

4

JAKE PARKER

"Who the hell is Nella, and why do we need her help?" Gus asked, leaning back in his chair, crossing his tattooed-covered arms over his barrel chest.

Yeah, I could totally see him in prison. Not that I knew any other ex-cons.

But I did know I wouldn't want to be on that man's bad side.

"Nella is Bud Bryson's daughter. You know, your employer? The namesake of Bryson's Garage, where we work? Since he's all laid up with a smashed leg, he got her to come back and run the garage."

My stomach had sunk the moment Sebastian

mentioned Nella, and now that I'd learned she was not only coming back to town but would also be running my place of employment, I had to set down my can of Coke. My jaw clenched so hard I couldn't drink any more, anyway.

I tried to relax.

But it wasn't working. I was royally fucked.

Sebastian continued—for Gus's sake. I already knew all I needed to.

"Look, Nella practically grew up in this garage, just like I did. She knows her shit," he explained.

Gus rolled his eyes. "Well, is she at least hot?"

At this, Sebastian turned to me.

"And even more importantly," Gus interrupted, "did you ever… you know, *do* her?"

I was not looking forward to this part of the conversation.

Sebastian frowned and shook his head. "Dude, she's my best friend's little sister. He would have killed me, and as you can see, I am still standing."

"Then why isn't big brother here, taking over?" Gus asked.

"Robbie left town a long time ago. He doesn't come back. He just doesn't."

Gus threw him a strange look. I didn't blame him. On the surface, it was a little odd that the oldest son wasn't coming back to help his dad.

But then, Robbie was a little odd. At least compared to other people from our little town. He was one of those guys who left and didn't look back. Shit, he probably even lied about being from here.

I felt for Sebastian, though. They'd been the best of friends all their lives until high school graduation. Robbie left town shortly thereafter, and even when he did come back after getting kicked out of college, had no time for any of his old friends. He was on a mission to get his shit together so he'd never have to come back.

We'd see if Nella was the same. After all, she'd decamped to New York City in recent years, just like her older brother. I didn't know about anybody else, but I'd heard nothing about her except the very occasional update from her best friend and town gossip, Izzy.

"So did *you* do her?" Gus asked, grinning at me.

His question snapped me out of my reverie.

"What? Me? Why are you asking?"

He looked between Sebastian and me. "Because Seb here threw you a look. And I know that looks screams history…"

Nosy fucker.

"Share how you know her. Or should I say *how well* you know her?" Sebastian said.

Goddammit. There was no privacy in this damn place.

I threw my hands up. "Whatever, man. We got together in high school. Anything else you want to know?"

Gus leaned forward in his chair, the buttons of his garage shirt straining. "Why so sensitive, buddy? There's obviously more to the story."

Sebastian sighed and rolled his eyes. "He slept with her and then told the whole school. Her rep was trashed for quite a while."

"That's bullshit!" I snapped. "Why don't you make sure you know your facts before you start flapping your gums."

Asshole. They both were.

"Well, set us straight, Jake. What's your side of the story?" Sebastian asked.

I was saying no more. There just wasn't any good to come out of it.

"Don't worry about what's not your business. What's important now is that I am about to be out of a job. No way is Nella keeping my ass around this place. Fuck."

I looked down at my filthy fingernails. Just when I thought I could split this little town myself and finally get my ass to college, something comes along and mucks up my plan. Never fails. I had a decent job at Bryson's Garage as assistant mechanic. Bud was good to me, and let me know I had a future at the place if I wanted it. He paid me enough to put some money aside for college. I'd been waiting since I was eighteen—seven long years—to attend State. I'd thought it was all within reach.

Better late than never, right?

Even though I'd been a good student, I'd always assumed I wasn't going to college. It was just not the kind of thing a kid like me did, coming from a family like mine, which didn't have two nickels to scratch together. But over the years, I realized there was no reason I shouldn't go. Problem was, I didn't have the grades for scholarships, and my parents' money situation was sure as hell not going to change.

So here I was, getting ready to pull the trigger, when Bud goes and falls off a freaking ladder, and Nella's on her way home.

Who knew my existence—and my dreams—were so flimsy? Just one broken bone away from massive implosion.

Fuck.

I slapped my hand on my thigh. "It's been nice knowing you guys."

I wondered if I should clean out my locker right away, or wait until the axe actually fell.

But Gus didn't seem to think it was all that bad.

Compared to what he went through, I supposed it wasn't.

I mean, it wasn't like I was facing prison, or anything like that.

But still.

"Dude," he started, "you're both adults now. Even women don't hold grudges that long," he laughed.

Easy for him to say. He'd never met Nella Bryson.

5

NELLA BRYSON

"How'd it happen?"

My father looked at me like he didn't know what I was talking about.

So, I repeated myself.

"Dad. How'd you fall off the ladder? You know, and break your leg?"

He slapped his hand on the hospital bed and looked up at the ceiling in frustration. "I *told* you. Cleaning leaves out of the gutters. Happy belated birthday, by the way."

Right. Okay. He didn't want to talk about the fall. But the strange thing was, there were no trees in our yard taller the house. So, how would the gutters be full of leaves? I could see the occasional leaf blowing in, maybe from a neighbor's yard. Maybe dropped in the gutter by a bird. But to the extent that they needed a full-on cleaning? Something wasn't adding up.

On the other hand, what did I know about home maintenance? I lived in a fifth-floor walkup in New York city. The closest I got to working with nature was chasing away cockroaches.

"When it happened, Dad, how'd you get help? Did you have your phone on you? Did you call 911, or call for the neighbors?"

I knew I was pressing my luck, but I had to know.

He looked out his hospital room window, as if he were barely listening. Guess the pain meds were kicking in. Or not.

Thus, the grouchiness.

"Oh, um. I got a ride to the ER."

Okay. So much for my line of questioning. For now. If he didn't want to talk about the accident, that was fine. I guess it didn't matter *how* it happened anyway—just that it *did*.

Although the evasiveness, if that's what it was, seemed awfully strange.

"So, Dad, I'll be here in town for a couple days to

help you out. Then I'll catch the bus back to New York."

His head snapped in my direction. I finally had his attention.

"A couple days? What do you mean? Didn't Robbie tell you?"

Robbie-who-wanted-to-be Robert? Mister New York attorney who just made partner? *That* Robbie?

He'd told me all I needed to know—that his job and life were far more important than mine, and because of that, I could leave New York at the drop of a hat and suffer no consequences because there was nothing really consequential about my life.

"Yeah, Dad, he filled me in."

"I'm not sure he did, honey."

I frowned. "What? What am I missing here?"

Dad shifted in his bed, and for the first time since I'd arrived, he looked a little uncomfortable. I wasn't sure if it was his leg, or whatever he needed to talk to me about.

"Nella, I'm not going to be back up on my feet for a while."

"Okay. I figured that. But you'll just use crutches, right?"

He took a sip of water and laid his head back on his pillow. "See this leg right here, Nella?"

"Yes, I do, Dad."

"This is a very bad break. I'm gonna be laid up for a long time. They don't know when I'll even be able to use crutches."

The reality of the situation started to sink in. No wonder my jerk brother didn't want to be bothered. He knew that once he got here, there would be no leaving.

"I see. I hadn't realized it was that bad."

Robbie had set me up.

Dad nodded. "I'm sorry, honey. But I'm going to need you to stay for a while and run the garage."

Um, what?

"Dad, I can't do that, I don't know how—"

"You have to, Nella. And you are perfectly capable. Look, this is a family business. It was started by my father, and I've labored in it since I was twelve years old. Neither of you kids wanted to take it over. Which is fine, I guess, but I worked all those years to build it for what? Tell me, Nella, for what?"

"Um... I don't know... I'm sorry Dad, it just wasn't for me—"

I thought pain meds were supposed to put you in a good mood. Maybe I could talk to the nurse about upping his dose.

And because of his crankiness, it didn't seem like a good time to discuss how the garage was dirty and smelly, and while I may have hung out there when I was a kid, I'd lost my desire for the place a long, long time ago.

I understood his being concerned about the garage. It was his baby. It had been a family affair, at least for a period of time. When my mother was alive, she even handled the bookkeeping. And my after-school job in high school included ordering supplies and car parts. I'd even put his inventory on a spreadsheet once I'd learned Excel.

It had been a good time. My best friend Izzy thought I was super cool because I had a job and money, *and* got to be around Sebastian, my brother's foxy best friend, who also worked at the shop.

This was serious currency for a teenager.

But that was a long time ago, and I could no longer hang out at Dad's shop like an underpaid groupie. I had a job and an apartment and rent to pay in New York. What was I supposed to do about all that?

Further, I no longer had any idea how Dad ran things. It had been years since I'd worked with him. I was sure his systems were different, just like cars were.

I was sure I'd be of no value, aside from just being there to watch over things in his absence.

Was that what he wanted? A baby-sitter?

"Dad, is Seb still working for you? Why don't you

have him take over? What about the other mechanics?"

I hadn't seen Sebastian, my brother's best childhood friend, in years. Could he still possibly be as handsome as he once had been?

Sebastian was dad's right-hand man. I'd always figured he was *heir apparent* to the shop since neither my brother nor I wanted it. God knew he deserved it. He'd been a loyal employee since before he was old enough to legally work, paid under the table by my father.

But Dad shook his head. "No. I only trust my money to family."

I rolled my eyes, which turned out to be a big mistake. "But Dad, he's like your second son—"

This time, he slammed his hand down on the hospital bed railing, the resulting racket startling the shit out of me.

A drowsy nurse poked her head into Dad's room. "Everything okay here, Mr. Bryson?" she asked, sighing.

"Yes, yes, we're fine," he snapped.

Jesus. I hadn't expected him to get so upset, I guess because I hadn't realized how important it was that I be there.

I mean, if he needed me that badly, I guessed I was going to stick around. End of discussion.

Even though the thought of it made my stomach churn.

Jesus. What would I do in this Podunk little town? I mean, my best friend Izzy was still here, pumping out baby after baby. I doubted seeing her would be enough to fill my social calendar.

Guess I'd be watching a lot of Netflix.

And what would I do about my job and apartment back in New York?

I put my hand on my father's arm. "Dad, I'm here for you. I've got you covered."

He studied me for a moment, then exhaled a long breath. "Thanks, sweetie. I knew I could count on you. And goddamn, if you don't look more like your mother every time I see you."

I'd take that as a compliment. Mom was a looker.

But back to business. "Now tell me, Dad, who else works at the shop these days? Who are your mechanics?"

He pushed himself up a little in bed, excited to talk about the business.

"Well, in addition to Seb, who you know, I've also got Jake Parker—"

"J... Jake? Would that be a different Jake Parker than the one I went to high school with? Or the... same?" My voice trailed off.

My stomach suddenly didn't feel so well.

Especially when Dad looked at me like I was crazy, which answered my question. "Of course, he's the same one you went to high school with. What other Jake Parker is there?"

"Right. Of course."

This was not good.

"Um, who else do you have?" I squeaked, clearing my throat, now terribly dry.

"Honey, do you need some water?" He handed me a cup from the table next to his bed.

"In addition to Seb and your old classmate Jake," he continued, "I have a guy who's been with us for only a few months, Gus Martins. He's a hard worker. Does damn good work."

He nodded happily, obviously pleased with his hiring choice.

I took a gulp of the water he'd passed me. "Cool, Dad. And how did you find him?"

"Well, you know that program with the state prison, where you can hire newly released men to help them out? Give them a fresh start?"

I couldn't say I was familiar with that program.

And had my dad just said the word *prison*?

"Gus was in the slammer for ten years for involuntary manslaughter. He's out now and I have to say he's doing fantastic."

The new guy... had been in prison? For manslaughter?

Didn't manslaughter also mean murder? As in, killing another human being?

I didn't care how good he was at fixing cars if he was also good at murdering people.

Great. Just fucking great. The guy who ruined my life in high school, *and* an ex-con were about to be part of my day-to-day existence, as well as my brother's best friend who'd I'd followed like a love-sick puppy all my childhood.

Things were off to a great start.

6

———————

NELLA BRYSON

I GRABBED THE KEY FROM UNDER THE DOOR MAT, AND let myself into my dad's house. Well, I guess it was my house too. Or was it?

I hadn't lived there in seven years, having split right after high school.

But when I entered, it sure felt like my house. From what I could see, everything was the same. The coat rack Dad had found at a flea market stood in the corner, the bowl of plastic fruit I'd gotten Mom for some holiday was on the dining room table, and the same carpet runner I'd once spilled bong water on covered the stairs. Even the stain was still there.

The only real difference was the layer of dust on everything. And piles of newspapers. Everywhere.

Not to mention the nearly thread-bare carpet, broken window pane in the kitchen, and empty beer cans on the coffee table.

The same but different.

When my mom was alive, she kept things like this under control. When she passed, the three of us tried to keep the house clean. Sometimes we succeeded, sometimes we didn't.

But Dad didn't have the sensibilities Robbie and I did. He let the place get dirty, not because he was lazy or didn't want to clean—he just didn't see the dirt.

I made my way upstairs to drop things in my old room, which was, like the rest of the house, the same except for a layer of dust and general fading. Same for Robbie's room, just next door. The bathroom held the now-ratty towels my mother had proudly gotten on sale at Macy's shortly before she passed away, and it didn't look like Dad had put up a new shower curtain in several years.

Needless to say, my parents' bedroom was the same. The Laura Ashley comforter Mom found at an outlet store, also a little worse for the wear, was neatly placed on the bed. Dad had always been a stickler for making beds.

I slowly walked toward their closet and first opened Dad's side, which, no matter how hard anyone tried to eliminate it, always smelled slightly of the garage. It was nothing terrible or offensive, just a low-key motor oil and grease scent.

When I moved to my mother's side of the closet, my hand rested on the knob of the louvered doors. Would there be anything on the other side?

When I'd last looked, and it had been years, Dad had not removed any of Mom's things. He just couldn't bear it. I didn't blame him. Her cancer came on suddenly as did her passing, and it had left all of us reeling. He'd clung to the little she'd left behind.

I finally pulled the doors open and found that Mom's dresses, slacks, and flowered blouses were exactly where they'd been hanging since she'd left us ten years before, when I was only fifteen.

And it hit me, a wave of overwhelming memories.

Her scent. There it was. Her beautiful, clean, favorite, L'Air du Temps cologne, was permanently steeped into everything she wore.

I stepped into the closet until my nose pressed against her things, and took a deep inhale. I let my fingers run along the fabric of her blouses, and it was as if she were right there in front of me, giving me cookies after school, taking me to the diner for a chocolate-chocolate milkshake, or scolding me for being sassy.

And I was finally glad I'd come, if not home, then at least back to the house I'd grown up in.

7

GUS MARTINS

"Glad you could make it."

Sebastian glanced up at me, elbows deep in the engine of an old Cadillac belonging to a local judge.

"Sorry, man," I said, buttoning up my garage shirt. "I got some bad news this morning."

The senior mechanic straightened up and set his tools down. "Yeah? What kind of bad news?"

It was par for the course if you were an ex-con. Shit fell on my head on a regular basis.

"The landlady found out about my prison time and freaked. Said I should have told her, and now she doesn't feel safe with me around. Meanwhile, her boyfriend is a drunken bum who yells at her day and night. But I'm the one who's gotta leave."

Sebastian wrinkled his brow. "What? You have a lease, right? She can't just kick you out. Tell her to go to hell."

He picked up his tools and dove back into the Caddy.

"You're partially right, Seb. She's the one who didn't run a background check until I'd been living in the place for a while, and someone in town told her about me. So she finds out and freaks, telling me I'm not the person I told her I was."

"And?"

"On that basis, she can kick my ass out. If I protest, she'll just formally evict me."

I knew it was too good to be true that I was accepted to the first apartment I'd applied for. In addition to that, Bud had hired me without hesitation, partially because he got a tax break for hiring a convicted felon, but also because he gave me a tricky repair to work on and I aced it in half the time he'd expected.

My soon-to-be-ex-apartment was nothing to look at—a basement unit in a crappy little house that was already furnished with junk other tenants had left behind over the years. But it was all mine, a huge improvement over prison. Bud had sold me an old pickup truck he had on the lot, which I fixed up just well enough to get me back and forth to work. I was repaying him with monthly installments. That had been his idea, bless him.

So, if the landlady was the only one on my ass, maybe I shouldn't be complaining. I knew guys getting out of prison who didn't have a goddamn thing going for them. No family, no program to help them get back on their feet, and no prospects.

That could have been me. Easily.

I grabbed a work order and some keys to get going on the next car in line. "It sucks Seb, how people hold prison time against you. It's part of the price to be paid, I guess. Like a gift that keeps on giving. I'd thought that once I was out, serving time would be behind me. But in some ways, it's the same bullshit, just different."

I had no right to bellyache, as resentful as I was for being put away for as long as I was. But I'd learned my lesson the hard way.

Next time I see a bar fight and am tempted to jump in to help break it up? Rather than slugging someone, who might fall down and hit his head and die because of it, I'm fucking walking away. No more trying to help.

I lost ten years of my life paying for that lesson.

The funny thing was, I thought if there were ever

any trouble with my apartment, it would be over how I'd smuggled a cat in when pets were not allowed. Actually, I was now up to two cats. I couldn't help but take in the poor creatures when they had nowhere else to go. But the landlady never even figured out I had cats.

But she sure as hell found out about my time in prison.

"Gus, you could probably crash on the sofa here for a while if you had to. We have a shower in the break room, as you know. I think you'd be all set," Sebastian said.

Bud would probably be fine with something like that, in fact he'd probably even suggest it if he knew of my predicament.

But I didn't want to wear out my welcome. The man had already done so much for me.

"Hey, man," Jake called from the other bay, "anyone want to go for coffee? Like, real coffee? Not the swill we have here in the office?"

Sebastian wiped the sweat off his forehead. "I could totally go for coffee. Gus, do you mind watching things?"

"All good, guys," I said, diving back into the SUV I was working on as the guys left.

With a few minutes to myself, I cranked up the stereo to a Metallica station and got lost in my work.

That's what I loved about being a mechanic. It was a non-stop puzzle of deciphering problems, and creating solutions to them, and could occupy my brain for hours.

I liked everything about cars. They'd fascinated me as a kid, and when the prison offered automotive mechanics courses, I was the first to sign up. I figured that whatever else was going on in my life, I'd always have work.

People loved their fucking cars, right?

The guys who passed up the opportunity to learn a trade like this? Completely out of their gourds.

Guess they wanted to bag groceries for the rest of their lives.

"Excuse me. *Excuse me*," a voice hollered over my head-banging music.

I saw a woman out of the corner of my eye, and clicked the music off.

I grabbed a rag to wipe my hands and approached her. "Apologies, miss. Got a little carried away."

The corner of her mouth extended in a fake smile, and I realized I could either try to win her over, or hustle her the hell out.

I chose winning her over because she was fucking beautiful. Her shiny jet-black hair and glittery blue eyes socked me right in the gut. I'd been out of the slammer for several months, but hadn't even really tried dating yet.

And every time I saw a looker, I was reminded of that.

I ushered the woman back to our front office, and decided to have a little fun. If I couldn't meet women at the garage, where would I?

"How can we service you today, miss?" I asked.

Her brows rose. "Excuse me? What was that?"

I leaned a little closer and damn if she didn't smell delicious, wearing some sort of old-fashioned perfume that contrasted perfectly with her spunky rockabilly look.

"I said… we're full service here, and can take care of all your needs."

She was either going to storm out, slap my face, or get my drift. And with Bud out of the office, as awesome as he was, I felt free to have a little fun.

"Um… um…" she sputtered, looking over my tattooed arms and shaved head.

That's right baby. I am fucking here for you.

Before she could gather her thoughts, I continued. "What can I *do* to you—I mean *for* you, today?"

Crossing her arms, she looked me up and down. "I was thinking—"

The bell on the front door rang, interrupting her.

"Oh my god, look who it is," Sebastian bellowed

as he blew in the door, setting down the two cups of coffee he was holding.

The woman whipped around and squealed, jumping into his arms.

"Nella, you look amazing!" he said, twirling her around. "How long has it been? Five years?"

Nella? Had he said *Nella?*

As in Nella Bryson?

As in the daughter of Bud Bryson, who owns Bryson's Garage, who was also my boss?

Whom I just been flirting with like a horny, desperate teenage virgin?

She giggled and jumped up and down in her combat boots. "Something like that. God, it's good to see you, Seb. Things have been pretty… crazy."

Great. I'd just been coming on to the boss's daughter. Of all the fucking women in this town, I had to pick the one who was, essentially, my *boss*.

Not only was I about to lose my housing, but my ass was getting fired, too.

8

GUS MARTINS

"So that's Nella?" I asked Jake, gesturing toward the office where she and Sebastian continued their happy reunion.

I'd slipped away carefully. And quietly.

Maybe she'd forget.

No, scratch that. Women never forget. I'd always be the shop douchebag.

Jake nodded resignedly and sighed. "The one and only. When Seb and I returned with the coffee, I headed straight in here instead of the office. I'm sure you noticed, and I'm sure Nella noticed. How would she not? I know at some point I'll have to talk to her, but I prefer to salvage my job for as long as I can."

"You and me both, brother. I seriously stuck my foot in my mouth by flirting with her before I realized who she was. I mean, how did Bud produce a daughter like that? She's gorgeous. Combination punk and rockabilly chick. Just how I like 'em. And that tight little T-shirt she's wearing—"

Jake held his hands up. "Gus, you gotta stop talking like that right now. You gotta stop thinking like that, too, with your little head. No good will come of it, especially if you want to keep your job."

I peered around the corner to get another look at the boss's daughter. "Oh, I'm pretty sure I've already lost my job. She'll fire my ass first chance she gets."

"That makes two of us, then. I told you how she hates me. We'll both be out of jobs. They'll be looking for new mechanics Monday."

"Why didn't you warn me?" I asked.

"Warn you of what?"

"How gorgeous she is. You could have said something. There are plenty of pretty women in this town. I just assumed she was one of them. Never thought she'd be *the* Nella Bryson of Bryson's Garage. Since when does a chick like that work in our business? She looks like she should be lead singer in a band. And to her credit, she kind of played along with my attempts to hit on her. Gotta respect that in a woman. You know, not losing her shit."

Jake slammed the hood on the car he was working on and wiped his hands down his jeans. "I haven't seen her in years and didn't really get a good look at her just now when I ran off like a damn pussy. She looks hot, huh?"

"Hot enough to get me fired. Dude, are you blind? Go take a look," I said, pointing.

He craned his neck toward the office. "Nah. I'll have to talk to her soon enough. I'm lying low for as long as possible."

I could see he was dying to check her out. But his drive for self-preservation was stronger. Smart guy.

Jake laid a hand on my arm. "You need to relax, Gus. *You'll* be fine. You *could* be like me—the dick who took her virginity and let word spread all over school."

Oh damn. That's a pretty big fucking offense. No wonder the guy was worried about his job. He had every reason to be.

In fact, I'd say he was more fucked than I was.

What a day, and it wasn't even ten a.m. yet. I hadn't done something so dumb since the day I tried to break up a fight and ended up in prison for ten years.

I might not end up back in prison this time, but I wasn't sure that where I *was* headed would be any better.

9

NELLA BRYSON

That had been awkward.

Painfully awkward.

First, the ex-con, Gus, was working it like I was the last woman on earth. I could kind of understand it if he'd been locked up as long as my dad had said. I was going through a pretty rough dry spell, myself. But shit, that man dug himself in *deep*.

The dictionary definition of 'blue balls.'

The dictionary definition of 'convict,' too.

That's how tough he looked.

With his shaved head, huge biceps straining the sleeves of his shirt, and tattoos on almost every bit of exposed skin, he was the quintessential prison inmate, at least according to what I'd seen in movies.

I wouldn't be too happy about running into him in a dark alley.

And yet, despite the hefty intimidation factor, the way he looked at me sent shivers down my spine. It was like he was looking *into* me, and that he knew things I would have preferred to keep to myself. I'd wanted to tear my gaze away from him, but somehow, couldn't, at least not until Sebastian arrived and broke the spell.

Gus was the kind of alpha male women fantasized about, who knew what he wanted and took it, leaving them wanting more.

But at the same time his gaze drilled me straight to my core, his eyes crinkled with his smile, something both charming and disarming at the same time.

How the hell did he do that?

He somehow came off as Mister Macho, but made you laugh at the same time.

And now the man worked for me?

Our interaction was, thankfully, brief. Sebastian, my 'brother from another mother,' had saved us both before we made fools of ourselves.

And it was so good to see Sebastian. I'd pretty much grown up with the guy, who'd been my brother's best friend before Robbie blew town and pretended like the rest of us didn't exist.

I mean, I'd left town, too, but at least I acknowledged the 'old gang.' My brother acted like his friends were dead.

"You hear anything from your brother?" Sebastian asked, clearly out of obligation.

I shrugged, suspecting how Robbie had probably hurt him like everyone else. At the same time, my father treated Sebastian like a second son, so even if his best friend had bailed on him, at least the father he'd never had hadn't turned his back on him.

Because I was young when everything went down, I didn't know the details of how Sebastian came to be absorbed into my family. He was just always there and all I knew was that 'there were problems in his home,' whatever that meant.

Weren't there problems in every home?

But my mom doted on him just like she did Robbie and me, and my dad taught him all about the automotive repair business. In fact, Sebastian had never worked anywhere besides Bryson's Garage, going back to when he was fourteen or fifteen years old.

I considered how I might answer his question about my brother, and decided to stay neutral. "Um, Robbie is Robbie, ya know?" I said, trying to make light of my brother's painfully obvious absence from everyone's lives.

What would be the point of telling him how Robbie had dismissed my existence and pretty much decided for the two of us that I'd be the one to 'come home' to help out dad?

Or that his promotion to law firm partner had exponentially fed his bottomless pit of self-importance, as if that were even possible?

I didn't want to make my brother look like more of a jerk than he already made himself.

Sebastian nodded, knowingly. And damn if he hadn't gotten more handsome since the last time I'd seen him, like I'd been afraid he might have.

He was always good-looking, and when I was a kid, I'd had a massive crush on him. That was how I came to know a bit about my father's business. I didn't particularly love cars, but I sure acted like I did whenever Sebastian was around—because when he was hanging out in the shop, I was right there too. Pretending, of course, that I was there to learn about engines and such.

But I was really there to brush up against him, ask stupid questions, admire the grime under his fingernails—you name it. There was nothing about him I wasn't enamored with.

And now, years later, he was even better-looking

with a bit of crinkling around the eyes and touch of gray in his sideburns.

My childhood crush long over, I now just had a ton of admiration for the man he was.

At least, I thought the crush was behind me.

Then there was *Jake*.

My high school heartbreak. I'd spotted him as he and Sebastian returned with their coffee. The moment he'd laid eyes on me, he bypassed the office by detouring directly to the garage. I didn't blame him. I'd be afraid of me too if I'd fucked up like he had.

We'd been sweet on each other for as long as I could remember. In elementary school, he'd slap my butt when no one was looking. When we got to middle school, he pretty much ignored me even though I caught him staring all the time. When high school rolled around, we each had a little more confidence, and started doing things together—just as friends, of course.

But high school had brought new pressures including raging hormones, and the feeling that everyone around us was already having sex.

If I had only known that most of the kids claiming to be 'sexperts' were actually big liars, and that the ones who *were* doing the deed were clumsy and inexperienced, I would have felt a lot less stressed.

But I didn't learn that until later.

Everyone in town knew the couple places you could go and make out in cars without being bothered by adults. If you were desperate, you could always hide in the woods. The local cops were too lazy to look there.

One night Jake and I went skinny dipping in a swampy little pond on the edge of town. It was not really lovely or romantic, but it gave us an excuse to take our clothes off.

And we all know what that led to.

I was thrilled to have finally lost my virginity, as unimpressive as the experience had been. I'd finally caught up to my best friend, Izzy, who'd been having sex for two years before I did the deed. I felt a little less like I was on the outside looking in.

But within days, I was getting looks in the school hallway, and when I walked through the cafeteria, I could hear the whispers.

I wasn't sure what I had done wrong, but more importantly, how the hell everyone found out.

And why they gave a shit.

But that didn't matter. What did, was that I was the talk of the school—that was until some other young woman decided to lose her virginity to some fucker who talked.

It was always the girls who were shamed. Never the boys. Obviously, they were doing it too, but the shit of it was that no one talked about them.

I'd held my head up and survived. But the pain of betrayal, and accompanying humiliation, devastated me.

I smiled through it all, and after graduation, I left town for college.

And now I was going to work with him.

The high school heartbreak, brother's best friend, and ex-con were now part of my day-to-day existence.

I was so not ready for this.

So I told them I was taking off, and headed home. Or to my dad's house. Whichever it was.

10

NELLA BRYSON

Not only was the inside of my father's house a mess, but so was the outside. In fact, the ladder Dad had been climbing when he had his accident was splayed on the ground, I supposed where it had fallen the day he got hurt.

Finishing the job he'd started seemed as good a place as any to begin, especially since there were still a few hours of daylight left. I leaned the ladder against the house to reach the first gutter.

But it was strange. As suspected, when I'd climbed to the top, I found there were no leaves in the gutters. I carefully looked around and confirmed something I already knew.

We didn't have any tall trees in our yard. Therefore, there were no leaves to fill up the gutters.

So what had dad been doing?

And why would he have lied, anyway?

"Hey. Hey, it's six o'clock," a woman called from across the street, arms crossed and smirking.

Shit. I remembered her. She'd lived there forever. Mrs... Starr. That was her name. Kind of a busybody, if I recalled.

"Hello," I called back, waving from my spot on the ladder.

Why had Mrs. Starr announced that it was six p.m.?

I looked at her again, and she pointed to her wrist, as if I might doubt her time-telling ability. Then she turned and waved to her next-door neighbor, a man who had come out with a ladder, and on the other side of her house, another man who'd come out with a ladder.

Were that many people cleaning their gutters?

Were these Stepford husbands, or something?

I had no idea what the hell was going on in my father's neighborhood, but realized I was starving so I began descending Dad's ladder when something caught my eye.

Dangling from the eaves was a small piece of black nylon strap. I reached to see what it was, but it wouldn't budge. With a bit more force, something hefty gave way, almost swinging me off the ladder.

Was this what had made my father fall when he wasn't cleaning the leaves he claimed to have been?

And because of the hefty weight on the other end of the strap, it nearly slipped from my fingers. But, risking falling just like my father had, I tightened my grip when I realized I had a big, heavy pair of binoculars swinging from my hand.

Huh?

I pulled them up and recognized them as the binoculars my dad had used over the years at sports events and to watch planes flying overhead.

What the hell were they doing on the roof of his house?

Before I continued my descent, I put them up to my eyes with one hand, the other holding the ladder, and looked around. I suddenly had a close-up of not only Mrs. Star, but the neighbors she'd waved at, now also on ladders and all looking in the same direction.

What the fuck?

I followed their gaze to the house right next door, to a second-story window that had no curtains or blinds.

And through that window was an attractive woman who looked like she'd just gotten home from exercising.

Who also happened to be undressing.

Like in, taking it all off.

A moment later, she was butt naked.

And the neighborhood husbands were watching.

Well, I was, too.

Was that what Dad had been doing?

Was my father, Bud Bryson, proud owner of Bryson's Garage, a pervy peeping tom?

Wasn't that sort of thing against the law?

I glanced over at Mrs. Star, who nodded back like *I told you so*.

I hustled down the ladder, almost falling twice, and when I got to the bottom, fell to my knees. But I pushed myself back up, threw the binoculars over one shoulder, and hoisted the ladder to half-drag, half-carry it to the garage.

I had to hide the evidence.

When had my life become such a dramatic shit show? God, I'd thought New York was intense.

But it was child's play compared to what I'd come back to.

11

SEBASTIAN GREER

"Are you sure this is what you want, Bud?"

My surrogate father looked at me from his hospital bed and nodded like he'd never been so sure of anything in his life. And I sure as hell wasn't going to question him further. For all the years I'd known him, he followed his gut on nearly everything and amazingly was usually spot-on with his judgment.

Just one of the many things I admired about the man.

Not that he was perfect. But in my eyes, he was pretty damn close.

But he didn't pay me to be his *yes man*. So I made

a point to let him know when I had a differing opinion, even though they rarely swayed his.

Bud pushed himself up on his elbows, wincing at the movement it caused in his shattered leg.

I still didn't understand what he'd been doing on a ladder, cleaning leaves out of his gutters. It wasn't the time of year for that task. But I figured I wouldn't bring it up again. Last time I had, he'd changed the subject.

Whatever.

I jumped to help. "What can I get you, Bud?"

I looked around and saw the only option I had was to get him a drink of water. So, I did, because I didn't know what else to do. I hated seeing the poor guy in pain.

He took a sip and leaned his head back on his pillow.

"Ugh. That's better, thanks. Who knew a messed-up leg could be so goddamn painful? All my years of working in the garage had never produced an injury that hurt like this."

After his pain subsided, we got back on track.

"Seb, you need to know that Nella's gonna be in town for a while. I won't be out of the woods with this leg thing for a long time. I'm told the rehab could take months and that I have to go to some special facility or something."

I hadn't realized he was that bad off.

I nodded in understanding. "Gotcha, Bud. I just want you to know that if you want me to, I am happy to step in and run the place. You know, if Nella is dying to get back to New York or something."

He paused for a moment, considering his words. He'd obviously already thought this through. "Look. If I could trust you with something confidential, I'd appreciate it."

He could trust me with anything. He knew that. I pretty much owed the man my life.

"Seb, I'd like to see Nella start taking on some responsibility. I know she's been in New York for a few years, and has obviously figured out how to get by there, but I'd like to see her start 'adulting,' as the kids say now."

He said 'adulting' using air quotes. I had to stifle my laugh at his effort to use the current slang.

He continued. "You know, I don't want her serving up coffee for the rest of her life."

"Sounds like a plan, Bud."

I was honestly glad to have her back. I didn't know about the other mechanics – Jake had long-ago done her wrong, and Gus had stuck his foot in his mouth the moment he met her—but that was their problem, not mine.

She was smart, had always been a hard worker from what I remembered of our growing-up years, and fuck if she hadn't turned out to be quite the beauty.

I mean, she'd always been cute, but now… what a head-turner she'd become with her short, swingy hair and bright red lipstick. You didn't see many women around our small town who looked like her.

Which could be a problem for her. Did she still fit in here? Would she be happy? Sure, Bud was arranging things so she'd be forced to stick around a while, but if it made her completely miserable, where was the justice in that, all 'adulting' lessons aside?

"Seb, I'd appreciate if you could keep an eye on her, though. You know, look over her shoulder but so that she doesn't notice. I'd like her to feel success-ful. Build her confidence a little. She's not like her brother, Robbie, who just went out and conquered the world."

No, she wasn't like her brother. And that was a good thing. In his quest to 'get ahead,' he'd stepped on more than his fair share of toes. I didn't hold it against him—I knew he always wanted out of this town—but others were not as forgiving.

I got to my feet. It was getting close to opening

time at the garage and I wanted to honor Bud's wish that I support Nella any way I could.

"Whatever you need, Bud, just let me know. Hey, before I go, I've been meaning to ask you—do you need someone to go over and finish your gutters? Glad to help out, especially since you won't be home for a while."

He gave me a funny look. "I'm getting sleepy, Seb. Must be all the pain killers. I'll talk to you later."

With that, he closed his eyes and laid his head back on his pillow. He was still holding his cup of water, so I removed that from his hand and set it on the tray next to the bed. I pulled the soft blanket someone had brought him as a gift up to his chest and took one last look at him.

He was a funny guy. But I'd do anything for the man, just like he would for me.

12

SEBASTIAN GREER

I PULLED MY TRUCK INTO THE SMALL LOT AT THE garage and was surprised to see a car in my usual spot. Because we were short on spaces for employees, I pulled in right behind it.

As I got out of my truck, I passed Joe Walker coming out of the office, a shit-eating grin on his face.

"Hey, Seb," he said, avoiding my eyes.

"Morning, Joe. How're you?"

He nodded and picked up his pace. "Good man, good. Gotta run," he said, getting in his car and taking off.

Hmmm. Interesting. We'd had Joe's car pretty much held hostage for nearly a month because he wouldn't pay for his repairs. Said he was broke.

Problem was, Joe was always broke, and had stiffed the garage on more than one occasion. I hustled into the office where Nella was organizing the mess of papers Bud called his 'system,' and looked around for signs of Joe's supposed payment.

"Morning, Nella. Hey, did Joe Walker pay for his car? I just saw him drive off like a bat out of hell."

"Yes, he did," she sang, reaching into a desk drawer and waving around his check.

Oh shit.

Lesson number one, coming right up.

I rubbed the bridge of my nose between two fingers while thinking of the right way to tell Nella she'd messed up. Already. On Day One.

"Yeah, every check that asshole writes is rubber. As in they bounce all over the place. We only take cash from him."

Her smile faded. "Are you kidding me? How was I supposed to know that? I remember him from high school. He was always such a nice guy."

He was nice to Nella because he wanted to get into her pants. But he was a dick to everyone else.

I didn't mention that, though.

"He might have been a good guy in high school,

but he's now famous for being the local scammer. He owes money to every business in town."

We'd never see that money now. At least not until the jerk brought his car back and we were able to hold it hostage again. If he had any brains, he'd take his car out of town, to a garage that didn't know him, and rip *them* off.

I took a seat opposite Bud's desk—or should I say, now Nella's desk?—and ran my fingers through my hair, pulling it back into a small ponytail to keep it off my face.

"Nella, we hardly ever take checks anymore. Times have changed. We prefer cash, but also do debit and credit cards."

Tilting her head, she threw me the stink eye to end all stink eyes. "And I was supposed to know that, *how?*"

"Well, if you'd let me brief you first on how things have changed since the last time you were here—"

She leaned forward over her desk. Damn, she'd gotten feisty in recent years. "If you'd been here on time, this never would have happened."

I snapped back in my seat, thrown off by the vehemence in her tone. Was this an indication of what our working relationship was going to be like?

Not good.

I took a breath, hoping my calm would rub off on her. "First, Nella, there is a list on the wall right there, next to you, of the people who've passed bad checks at the shop."

She raised her eyebrows and turned to see where I was pointing. She looked up and down the wall at all the crap her father had stuck up there over the years, much of it faded with curling edges, and shook her head.

"What are you talking about? I don't see any list of bad check writers."

I got up and put my finger on Bud's list. "Right there."

She squinted. "You're kidding, right? I can barely read that. How the hell was I supposed to know that was there? And I'd need a magnifying glass to read it, in any case."

I went back to my seat. "That brings me to my second point, Nella. Your comment about my not being here on time was not cool."

She threw her hands up. "What? Were you here on time or not? It looked like you arrived at eight, to me. But we open at seven a.m.," she said, pointing at the sign on the door.

Ah. The source of the misunderstanding.

"Nella, that sticker's been on the door since we were kids. Your dad just never bothered to change it like a lot of other stuff around here," I said, pointing out the piles of paper and other junk he'd let accumulate on every surface.

She frowned. "So…?"

"So, I'm saying that Bud—your dad—changed our hours years ago. Everyone in town knows we open at eight. We just never updated the notice on the door, just like we never replaced the 'y' in the sign on the roof after that big storm fifteen years ago."

She dropped her head onto the back of her chair, and groaned. "Why the hell did he change our hours?"

"He said getting to work so early was inhumane and utter bullshit. End of discussion. Quote, unquote."

Actually, there'd been no discussion. And certainly no protest from me. After all, who didn't want to come to work an hour later in the morning?

"No offense, Nella, but you gotta get with the times."

The look on her face told me I could have chosen better words to let her know the business was run differently from when she was last hanging around.

I couldn't remember how long ago that had been —at least five years, probably more—but time marches on everywhere. Not just in New York City.

I mean, shit, we might be small town people, but that didn't mean *everything* stayed the same.

Nella certainly wasn't the same. She'd come home mature and incredibly beautiful, but sure wasn't happy to be running the show for Bud.

But if the man wanted her to succeed, then so did I. And I'd do anything to make sure that happened.

Even if it meant I had to struggle to keep my thoughts—and hands—to myself for the duration of her visit.

13

NELLA BRYSON

"Hello. Is Robbie there?"

I heard a long sigh at the other end of the line as my brother's put-upon admin realized it was me. And because I was nobody to Robbie, I was nobody to her.

"*Robert* is in a meeting."

God. She must love those five words.

I wondered if she was doing him too, that's how loyal she was to him.

"Charlotte"—at my use of her first name, I heard her gasp—"this is important. It has to do with… our father."

She sniffed. "I'm afraid, Miss Bryson, that Robert is in a meeting."

I still hadn't melted her cold heart. I supposed if I sent her roses and chocolates, she'd still be a snot.

"Are you sure there's no way you can cut in?"

Fingers drummed on a desk in the background, and I heard her breathing. That was it. Not even acknowledging my question.

Was I talking to an actual human? Because no human being could possibly be so horrid.

"Charlotte, go fuck yourself," I said, and hung up in her ear, then promptly texted my brother's cell. Again. And again, he didn't respond.

That witch couldn't possibly control his personal phone, could she?

Next, I called Mug Me, and when my friend Jelly came on the line, I was never so happy to hear a familiar voice.

In fact, I choked up.

"Hi, J… Jelly. I'm not sure when I'm c… coming back. But I will soon. I can't wait. I miss you and New York so much," I stammered.

"Nella? Are you okay?" she asked, alarmed.

"Mmmm-hmmm," I sniffed.

Truth was, I was over it. I was over Bryson's garage, and everything about it. I felt badly about my dad, but he didn't need me at the shop. His mechanics had everything under control and then some. They could run circles around me.

I couldn't touch anything there without somehow messing it up. And that included working with Sebastian, Jake, and Gus.

They didn't want me there. It was clear. And I didn't blame them. I didn't bring a damn thing to the table and to make things worse, I just got in the way.

Who wanted the boss's daughter watching over them, anyway?

And how the hell was I supposed to work with these guys? Sebastian, my brother's best friend, was my childhood crush. When I was twelve years old, I used to pretend-sign things with his last name, fantasizing that we'd someday get married.

That all ended when Robbie found my stash of notebooks and told everyone.

Jake, the guy I'd skinny dipped with and to whom I gave away my V-card was so afraid to speak to me that he ran in the opposite direction when he saw me. I didn't blame him for avoiding me, though. He knew he'd fucked up by bragging about doing it with me and ruining my reputation.

And last but not least, Gus, the burly ex-con, all tatted and shaved, with a scary-ass scar running through his eyebrow, who thought he could get into my pants the minute he saw me. Did I have 'do me' stamped across my forehead or something? And did working with him mean I'd have to feel his eyeballs burning into my backside every time I walked away from him?

There was no way this crazy arrangement of my father's could work. It was a disaster from the start, and though nobody's fault, I was set up to fail.

"Um, Nella, you don't sound fine," Jelly said when she heard me blow my nose.

"I… I'm coming back to New York. Can you tell me when I'm on the schedule next, so I can plan?"

A door closed softly in the background and I knew Jelly had stepped into the storage room, where we made all our personal phone calls.

"You're… you're coming back?" she asked.

"Yeah. I'm so psyched to see you."

She cleared her throat. "I'm psyched to see you too, sweetie. But you aren't on the schedule."

"What do you mean?"

She let out a long breath. "I'm not exactly sure, but I noticed your name's not listed any longer. So you can't sign up for shifts."

Huh?

"What? Why?"

"I'm… not sure. But I'll see if I can find out."

Jelly would figure things out. She was like that.

"But um, Nella? I... I think you may have been let go. Maybe they thought you weren't coming back."

What? My brother had told me that wouldn't happen.

"No way, I didn't tell them that at all. I said I would be back. Eventually. Are you sure it's not just a mistake?" I asked.

"How about I dig around a little? See what I can find out?" she offered. "Hey, Nella, my break's up. Let me get back to you."

And she was gone.

Did she know something I didn't?

Well, fuck that place. There were a shit-ton of coffee shops in Manhattan. I'd just find a job at another one.

Although I'd miss Mug Me. I mean, my friends were there and I could walk to work.

Next, I called my apartment. One of my roommates answered on the fifth ring, slightly winded. God, I hope they weren't doing it on my bed.

"Hey, it's Nella. I'll be back soon. Just gotta finish up a couple things here at my Dad's."

There was silence on the other end.

"Hello? You there?"

"Um, yeah, Nella. Say, we thought you weren't coming back. We've rented your room out."

Oh my god. Please say this wasn't happening.

First my brother didn't have time for me, then my job had flown out the window, and now I was homeless. What the fuck had I done to the universe to deserve this bullshit?

Cripes, the only thing left was for me to walk outside and be plowed into the earth by a falling meteor. It would be so fitting.

But I wasn't giving up yet. "You're kidding, right? You didn't rent out my goddamn room. All my things are still there."

Big sigh. "Actually… your things are in the building's basement. We packed them up for you though. For free. No charge," she said, like she was doing me a big favor.

What the fucking fuck?

I couldn't think of another thing to say, so I hung up.

14

NELLA BRYSON

"Everything okay, Nella?"

Did I look like everything was fucking okay?

After the news that I'd all but been kicked out of my scrappy but established life in New York City, I'd decided to clean that shitshow that was my father's office. There was nothing I liked as much as organization, and the clutter I was surrounded by was only adding to my anxiety. And if I couldn't scoot out of here as quickly and effortlessly as I'd thought I could, I needed to do something to make my days a little more bearable.

Not that I'd given up on New York. I'd get back

there somehow even if my own brother, job, and roommates had no interest in supporting me.

After finding a giant yellowed stack of invoices from various suppliers going back several years, I looked around for a shredder.

But why would I think Dad would have a shredder? Sebastian might think he'd modernized the business, but I knew my father well enough to know he'd do the bare minimum to avoid changing his routine.

Pulling open the bottom drawer in a rusty old file cabinet, I put a rubber band around the invoices to create a pile of things to get rid of later.

But as I stuffed them into the drawer, I noticed the corner of what looked like a Hallmark card caught in the way back, pinned by the cabinet.

Aside from being bent in a couple places, the envelope was in perfect condition. The outside of it read 'Bud.'

And the handwriting was my mother's.

It was funny, seeing her tidy script again. All the birthday cards, notes to teachers about being sick, and grocery lists came flooding back in a wave of emotion. I ran my finger over her writing, and slowly pulled the card out of the envelope.

It was for one of their anniversaries, with a cheesy photo of a loving couple in front of a roaring fire—like the other anniversary cards you see in the drugstores. I turned it over and saw it had cost three dollars.

That was a splurge on the part of my mom. She hated wasting money on things that would go straight into the trash.

But this one hadn't ended up in the trash. Dad had saved it.

I started to open the card to see Mom's inscription. But I stopped. I realized I didn't want to know what she'd written. It was personal, and Dad had treasured it enough to save it.

Like the way he'd saved everything of my mother's.

I slipped the card in my purse to bring to him, and buried my head in my hands.

Thanks, universe, for crapping on me and making me desperately miss my mom at the same time.

So when Sebastian entered the office and saw me in distress, he looked at me with the kind eyes that had bewitched me as a kid. My vision blurred with tears, like my emotions were just waiting to humiliate me in front of someone, but I was not going to cry in front of him. I'd have to hold off and explode later, in private.

"What's that?" he asked, watching me stuff the card into my purse.

I took a deep breath to control myself. "I found a card Mom gave to Dad. Obviously, a long time ago."

Shit, how old could that card be? Mom had been gone a good ten years…

"Your mom was a great lady, Nella. Just like you."

I laughed. "Yeah. Mom would have this place in tip-top shape in a matter of minutes. I don't even know where to start. I just fucked up by taking payment from that jerk, Walker, and can't make heads or tails out of anything. And I suppose you're here to tell me I messed something else up?"

I broke our gaze and looked down at Dad's desk. That was a shitty thing to say. But then, I felt pretty damn shitty.

Sebastian came around the side of the desk and propped his butt on a corner, sending yet another stack of papers fluttering to the ground.

Great.

"I… I came by to apologize, actually."

I looked up at him. Even seated, his height loomed over me. And he smelled good, like simple soap that somehow overrode the garage scent that had been part of my life since—well, forever.

I looked up at him, blinking away the couple tears I'd not managed to control.

And he reached down to catch one, wiping it clean away.

His touch sent such a jolt through me that I gripped the arms of my chair to hide it. But my inability to speak gave me away.

"I know this isn't easy for you, Nella. That you'd really rather not be here. And that your brother is no help at all."

At the mention of my brother, I snorted. I couldn't help it.

Sebastian laughed and nodded.

"But you know, this isn't easy for me, either," he added.

Um, what?

I gathered my wits back together. "Sorry, Seb, but I am calling bullshit on that. Everything is the same for you. Your life is stable. You have it all together. You're successful. My dad took you under his wing and you have the same job, home, friends—everything. You know how lucky you are? My life is a complete shit show. I mean, it wasn't that great before I left New York to come here, and now it's in a complete shambles. Did you know I've lost my job at the coffee shop and my roommates just kicked me out? All my shit is in the basement of our building, probably being run over by rats as we speak."

Ugh. I sounded like a whiny bitch. And to make

things worse, I had to look down at my lap to hide the new tears that fell from my eyes.

Fuck if I wasn't a major sad-sack.

"Okay. Fair enough. But how do you think I like Robbie's pain-in-the-ass little sister coming back to town all beautiful and grown up? If you don't think I've been dreaming of you every night since you got back, you are out of your mind."

This time, I really did grip the arms of my chair, because I was about to fall out of it.

Never in a million years would I have thought that's what Sebastian had on his mind.

Probably because I was too busy wallowing in my own crap to even consider someone else's.

"You… you think I'm beautiful?" I squeaked.

Dammit. I was not the type to dig for compliments. But there. I'd done it.

"You're hot as hell, too," he said.

Hot? Me?

"Serious?" I said in disbelief.

Sebastian dropped his head back and laughed. "Why the hell would I make something like that up? You know I'm not the type to blow smoke up someone's ass. I meant every word I said. Jesus."

With that, he got up off Dad's desk and started heading for the door.

But not before I grabbed his hand.

"Seb, you know why I always hung out here when I was a kid, right?"

Taking a step toward me, he nodded. "Of course. Everyone knew. You had a little crush. It was cute. But it's not cute anymore. You're fucking grown up and I can't stand it. You're Robbie's little sister. You're Bud's daughter. And I can't stop thinking about you."

"Okay then. Just shut up and kiss me."

The corner of his mouth quirked up, and he slowly lowered himself until our lips met.

I grabbed his thick arms so that my shaking knees couldn't fail me.

His kiss was soft at first, really not much more than brushing over my lips, teasing me with his warm breath. But in moments, he pulled me closer and pressed into me with an intimidating passion.

For the first time, we connected.

And, I had a feeling, not for the last.

15

JAKE PARKER

"HEY. CAN I COME IN?"

Nella looked up from whatever she was doing at her dad's desk, and when she realized it was me, scowled.

Shit. This wasn't going to be easy.

She gestured with her chin for me to enter.

Without uttering a word.

I took a seat, even though she didn't offer me one. "I saw you leave early yesterday, Nella, after your meeting with Seb."

Yeah, I was pretty much desperate to make conversation.

Her face softened a bit. "Yeah. I was, um… tired."

I nodded and looked around Bud's office. It was miles better-looking than before Nella had arrived. But I could see she had a long way to go.

"You're getting a lot done. I think it's been years since I've actually seen the surface of that table over there."

She sank down into her chair and laughed.

Was she finally relaxing?

Yes.

She pointed around the office. "I don't get my dad. I mean, I sort of get him. When my mom passed, this place became a mess."

It hadn't seemed to hurt him any.

"But he still kept the business running. I mean, he might have no organizational skills, but he figured out a system that worked."

She considered what I'd said. "Yeah. I guess. But this doesn't work for me. Messiness makes my skin crawl."

"I remember that about you," I blurted out before thinking.

Shit. I didn't want to start this way.

She shifted in her seat and folded her hands on her desk, all professional like. "So what can I do for you, Jake?"

Damn. That was icy.

I was just going to go for it. "Nella, it's time to clear the air."

She snorted. "Thirty-plus years of garage stench isn't going anywhere."

Okay. At least she could make a joke. That was a good sign.

"I, um… think you know what I'm talking about."

She just stared at me. Okay. She wasn't going to make it easy.

But I never thought it would be easy, getting back on track with her.

Shit, I never thought I'd have the chance. But ever since she'd gotten back into town, I'd been racking my brains about making things right between us.

And not just because she was now, essentially, my boss.

"Nella, I don't want there to be tension between us, and I want to lay it all out. We gotta talk, you know?"

She sat back in her chair, arms crossed.

That's what years of anger and resentment will do to you.

"I see. Well, I think you'd have more luck getting rid of the garage stench, in that case."

Fuck. I wanted to leave. Just drop the whole thing. Walk out and never return.

But something told me to keep pressing. I knew Nella, and I knew she was a reasonable person.

Well, at least she used to be. Before she went to New York.

I guess I had no idea what I was dealing with now. But I was pressing on.

"Can we… leave the past in the past, Nella? We're adults, right? And… to be honest, I'm worried about my job here. I need to keep it. I have a reputation in this town of being a good guy and don't want any… issues."

Fuck. That had come out all wrong. Like I was trying to make it about *me*, instead of the two of us.

"What I am trying to say, Nella, is—"

Leaning over the desk, she interrupted me with a raised hand. "That's interesting, Jake. Very interesting. Your concerns about your livelihood and reputation. I know a bit about those things. Especially losing a good reputation. If you remember, that's what happened to me in high school. Thanks to you."

She sat back in her chair, satisfied with her scolding.

"You know, Nella, I was not the one to spread rumors about you. Or talk about you. I never said a thing. I'd always wanted to tell you that, but you wouldn't give me the time of day."

She rolled her eyes. "How stupid do you think I

am? We fucked and two days later the entire school knew about it. Someone wrote 'easy' on my locker, for cripe's sake. People probably still say that about me behind my back, especially now that I'm back in town. Not that I'm staying here a minute longer than I have to…" She trailed off.

One thing about her hadn't changed. She was as goddamn stubborn as she'd ever been.

Part of the reason I'd always loved her.

Shit. Did I say love?

Like. I meant *like*.

"How long will you be here?" I asked.

To be honest, I'd hoped she wouldn't go running back to New York. That there would be enough here in town to keep her happy.

But I think I knew the answer to that.

"Well, considering my job and place to live are both gone, out the window, kaput, I expect I'll be stuck here longer than I want. At the very least, I have to wait until Dad's better. He really doesn't want me to leave. So there's that."

She looked around the office at the mess her father had left and the only way to describe the expression on her face was *bereft*.

Like she'd lost all hope.

The woman was seriously down in the dumps.

And I was trying to think of something I could say to help.

But I didn't get the chance.

"Jake, I appreciate your stopping by to talk. But I gotta get back to work. And I imagine you do, too."

I nodded and left, closing the office door quietly behind me, unsure of whether I felt better or worse than when I went in. And the future of my employment at Bryson's Garage felt as uncertain as ever.

16

JAKE PARKER

I SHOVED MY SORE FINGER IN A BAG OF FROZEN PEAS and lay back on my bed with a book. After the day I'd had, I was ready for some rest and relaxation.

Although hoping for quiet time when you live above a laundromat open until eleven p.m. isn't much more than that—hope. And because of the way my day had gone down, I hated my shithole apartment more than usual.

I wasn't sure which was the worst part of the day —seeing how freaking unhappy Nella was with me and her life in general—or smashing my finger with a wrench when fixing somebody's muffler.

On top of that, I was working on the car of some guy just passing through town, in a rush to get somewhere, so he stood at the edge of the garage telling me to hurry the entire time.

He had been breathing down my neck—literally looking over my shoulder—until Sebastian told him that for liability reasons, he had to stay out of the mechanics' work area.

I'd never heard that rule, but was glad Sebastian had come up with it.

The guy moved to the doorway but unfortunately never shut up and it was when I turned to him to hear the 'important' thing he was telling me that I crunched my finger.

Fucking thing hurt like hell, not that I let on. Minor injuries were common in my line of work, and you're labeled a wimp if you complained. I mean, shit, I'd seen guys practically bleeding to death before they'd agreed to medical help.

So for a sore finger, I had to wait until I got home to ice it. And it was now swollen and a nice shade of purple. Possibly even too late for the frozen peas to work their magic, but at least their numbing power dulled the pain.

My phone buzzed for the third time with a message from Izzy, who was trying to get a bunch of people together for beers. I'd been ignoring her texts, which was next to impossible because as a self-appointed 'social director' for my high school's graduating class, she never took no for an answer.

I usually showed up to her shindigs, even if it was just to make a brief appearance, because arguing with her about attending was futile.

But this time, I was pretty certain that Nella, as Izzy's best friend, would be there, and if there was anything that made staying home, reading and tending my sore finger appealing, it was that.

But it was her latest text message that got me.

get your ass here or i will remind everyone how you peed ur pants in second grade

Okay, that got me laughing, and, I had to say, it felt damn good. She was funny, that one. Unlike Nella, Izzy had married young and been pumping out the babies ever since, but was still as much a wild woman as she'd been when we were all sixteen.

I groaned when I pushed myself off the bed using the hand with the sore finger, and put the peas back in the freezer. It was probably as good a night as any to go out anyway, since it sounded like there was a party down in the laundromat and there'd be no sleep until much later.

I managed to tie my sneakers minus one working finger, and pulled on a jacket to walk down the street to the local bar.

Actually, the only bar we had.

When I arrived, the party was in full swing.

My graduating class never had reunions because we were always getting together, anyway. But maybe if we had, Nella would have come home more often.

Then again, maybe not.

I spotted her the moment I walked in, sitting at the bar, downing a shot.

Christ. I didn't think she was that kind of drinker.

"Hey, Nella. Whatcha drinking there?" I said, grabbing the stool next to her.

Her head whipped in my direction. She had a black smudge of makeup under one of her eyes, and she had to grab the bar for balance.

Damn. This was not good.

"Oh. It's you. The one who ruined my life," she said.

She was well on her way to a major bender. And she'd feel like shit the next day if she were still the person I thought she was.

I knew better than to try to talk sense into her, but when had I ever chosen the easy path? "Nella, your life was not ruined. Look at all the friends you have here. I wish you weren't so fixated on that."

Her head snapped back and she raised her

eyebrows indignantly. "Oh really? What do you know? You weren't labeled the town whore."

"I'm telling you, Nella, it wasn't me—"

"Then why were all the boys trying to sleep with me? Besides," she sniffed, waving the bartender over for a refill, "you weren't even that good."

"Wha... what?" I lowered my voice. "That was my first time just like it was yours. I was young and inexperienced. I'm... well... better now."

Was I really defending myself? Fucking pathetic.

"Yeah, right."

"She'll take a big glass of water," I to the bartender before he poured her another.

"Hey, where do you get off—" she started to protest.

I put my hand over hers, which instantly shut her up. "Let me prove it."

She pulled her hand back. "Prove what?"

"That I've learned. And that I can fuck you senseless if you let me," I whispered in her ear.

Her mouth dropped open and her pupils dilated. "Um... well, um..."

Ha. I'd finally shut her the hell up.

It was then that I glanced behind her and found Sebastian and Gus on the other side of the bar, nudging each other and laughing as they watched me try to reason with Nella.

Bastards, having a laugh at my expense.

Although I couldn't get too mad. After all, if the shoe were on the other foot, I'd be making the same dick move, laughing my ass off at them.

"Tomorrow night, Nella. I will pick you up and take you out."

Her mouth opened and closed a couple times but no sound came out.

"And right now, I'm taking you home and putting you to bed. You've had enough for one night."

I pulled some money out of my wallet and laid it on the bar. "C'mon. Let's go."

I hooked an arm around her waist as I walked her back to my place to get my car. She wasn't so far gone she really need assistance, but I was happy for an excuse to put my arm around her.

She still hadn't said a word after we'd arrived.

"What's up, Nella? Cat got your tongue?" I teased, opening the passenger side door for her.

She looked down at her hands and shrugged, having sobered up a bit. "Nah. Just a shitty day."

I hooked a finger under her chin, and she looked up at me. I knew I was taking a risk.

But I lowered my lips to hers for a quick kiss anyway, and she was as soft and delicious as that night when we were only sixteen years old.

17

NELLA BRYSON

"Hɪ, Dᴀᴅ."

I stopped short, only a couple steps into his hospital room, with the card I'd found from my mother in hand.

Sitting in the visitor chair, which had been pulled right next to Dad's hospital bed, was the woman from next door.

The one who the neighborhood men watched get undressed and walk around naked.

And whom I was pretty sure—like ninety-nine-point-nine percent pretty sure—Dad was watching when he had his little accident.

The   falling-off-the-ladder-leg-breaking accident.

Which necessitated my return to town and Bryson's Garage.

"Oh. Hello," I said.

The yoga teacher must have been twenty years my dad's junior, with long blonde hair, willowy limbs, and a make-up-free but flawless complexion.

She jumped to her feet, pressed her hands together, and did a little bow in my direction, all with a beatific smile.

"Namaste."

No. Fucking. Way.

I'd attended many a yoga class in New York, so I was all over that Namaste shit. But my dad? He was about the furthest thing from a yogi walking the planet. Even though he hadn't walked anywhere in a couple weeks.

"Bella Nella!" Dad boomed, using the nickname that had, until now, only been used in family settings.

Like *private* family settings.

He reached a hand in my direction and I have to say, looked so fucking happy it brought tears to my eyes.

"Hey, Dad," I said, stuffing Mom's card back in my purse.

"I want you to meet my next-door neighbor, Dakini."

Oh for god's sake. I was certain Dad had no idea that a Dakini was some sort of ancient female spirit —some would say demon—and that his neighbor had no doubt adopted the name, not likely having been given it at birth.

"Hello, Dakini," I said.

She smiled peacefully and turned back to Dad. "'ll let you two have your visit time. Bud, if you need anything, just give me a call, okay? We can continue our meditation tomorrow."

What? Meditation? My father?

He'd always thought meditation was quietly reading on the toilet.

Then, the unthinkable happened.

Dakini put her hands in a prayer position again and turned to my dad, who put his hands in a prayer position as well. They each bowed until their foreheads touched, took a deep breath, and said *Namaste.*

They came out of their bow, looked at each other adoringly, and Dakini floated out of the room, probably the same way she'd floated in.

And I stood at the end of my father's bed, unable to speak. Or move.

He signed happily. "She's a lovely lady, Nella. She brought me this blanket on the bed. It's been a life saver on lonely nights here in the hospital when I was longing for something familiar."

"Way to make me feel like shit, Dad," I mumbled.

"What was that, Nella?" he asked, a hand behind his ear for me to speak up.

But I wasn't going there. I had a job to do.

"So, Dad, are you ready? For me to take you to the rehab place?"

He clapped his hands together.

"Oh yeah. In fact, hell yeah." He lowered his voice and peered out the door. "I don't mean to sound like a complainer, but the food here really sucks."

"Well, Dad, this is a hospital. Not a resort. Guess they don't want you staying too long."

"True. So true. And I'm looking forward to change. New beginnings," he said, closing his eyes with a big sigh.

Okay. This was not the dad I grew up with. Not that I begrudged him any sort of growth.

"So how long will you be in rehab, Dad? Couple weeks? Is that what you told me?"

He dropped his head back on his pillow and laughed. "Oh no, Bella Nella. I'll be there one month, maybe even two."

He couldn't look happier about it.

It was all I could do, however, not to hyperventilate.

Two months? *Two* fucking months?

"Well, um, Dad, can't you, you know, do the rehab at home? And get a ride to the garage every day?"

"Mr. Bryson, you ready to go, sweetheart?"

I turned to find an officious-looking nurse in pink scrubs glance from Dad to me.

Maybe I could appeal to her. "Hi, hey, do you think the rehab really needs to be that long? You know, two months. I mean, that sound super excessive—"

"And who are you, miss?" she asked, looking me up and down.

"I'm his daughter."

"She's my daughter. Nella," Dad repeated proudly.

The nurse frowned. "I thought the *last* woman in here was your daughter."

I had to bite my tongue on that one.

The nurse took a couple steps toward the bed, hands on hips, and looked hard at Dad.

But he didn't realize he was in the company of the nurse from *Misery*. He was oblivious that this woman had designs on him at all.

Fuck me. When had Dad turned into a ladies' man?

He snorted. "Who? The blonde who just now left? Oh, she's my… neighbor."

Her face softened as she approached Dad. "I'll tell ya Mr. Bryson, we're sure going to miss you around here. We don't often get a patient as… pleasant as you."

She blushed. She actually blushed.

Jesus, maybe I should just leave the room a moment so she could profess her love.

It was all too much. And gross. This was my *Dad*. The man who fell asleep in front of the TV, snoring. Who still wore tighty-whities. And sometimes even socks with his sandals.

He was not the object of affection of… anyone. Well, until now.

"Um, excuse me. Back to the rehab thing please," I said with rising panic. "My father needs to get up and get walking. He has a business to run."

I glanced his way, and saw him frowning. Obviously, they'd brainwashed him into thinking he was an invalid.

"My dad… is a strong man. He doesn't need this bullshit hospital crap, nor the rehab that will probably cost him a fortune—"

"Honey, that's covered by insurance," he interrupted.

"Okay, Dad. That's great. But you need to just get up—"

Suddenly, the nurse's very strong grip was on my arm, propelling me out the door and into the hallway.

"I'm sorry, miss," she said. "You are causing a disturbance. If you don't leave right now, I'll have security escort you out."

I yanked my arm out of her grip. "You can't kick me out. I'm here to take my dad to rehab. The rehab which he doesn't need—"

She put her hands up in surrender. "All right, miss. You will have to leave. Please wait for your father by the front lobby entrance. Our security guard right here will... make sure you find your way."

The security guard and I walked in lockstep until we reached the front of the hospital. He opened the door for me and waited for me to pass through.

"Sorry about that back there," I said sheepishly. "I'm just having a hard... day."

"That's okay, miss. Everyone around here is having a bad day." He pulled the door closed and the hermetic seal of the hospital was gone. I was outside with traffic, ambulance sirens, and people asking guards for directions.

Well shit. I'd fucked that all up.

And it was clear New York was not in my near future. If it ever had been.

18

NELLA BRYSON

"Is this the same car you had in high school?"

"Yup," Jake said, putting the car in *drive* while I looked at the torn upholstery and cracked dashboard plastic.

"What's that bandage on your finger?"

He glanced at it like he'd forgotten it. "It's nothing."

Why was I doing this? Because I was fucking crazy? I was out for the evening with my sworn enemy.

And when he pulled up to the exact same wooded spot where I'd lost my V-card so many years before,

I thought I was going to scream. This guy was exactly the same as he was in high school.

"Have you grown up at all? Is this your best move? The one that got you into my pants almost ten years ago? Oh my god."

He turned the car off. "You know, Nella, you need to get over yourself. Sometimes you are so high and mighty—"

"What?" I exploded with all the fury I'd been feeling that week. "You bring me back here, like we're sixteen years old and are going to skinny dip again. You've got to be kidding me."

I crossed my arms and sank down in my seat.

"So… now that you're the big city girl, you're too good to skinny dip? Too good for us small town folks?"

I looked at him in the moonlight filtering through the trees, his profile perfect as it had always been.

Actually, he was even better looking than the last time I'd last seen him, dammit. Time had granted him a quiet maturity with a few crinkles on the sides of his eyes, and a more strongly defined jaw.

But all that didn't matter. What did was that I was wasting my damn time.

"I'm not saying I'm too good—"

But before I could finish, he was out of the car,

walking down to the pond we'd swum in so many years before.

So I jumped out after him. "Go ahead," I called. "Go swimming by yourself. Have fun!" I hollered, trudging through the trees to the swimming hole I'd not laid eyes on in a very long time.

And from where I stood, I watched Jake kick his shoes aside and peel off his polo shirt. I inched closer for a better look, and in the moonlight, I was struck by how buff he was. But when he yanked down his jeans and boxers and I got a look at his muscular ass, I realized he'd matured in other ways.

He glanced over his shoulder at me, then waded into the pond. When he got to the middle, he started treading water.

"Feels great. Shame you're too stuck on yourself to enjoy it," he called, splashing around.

"You know, Nella. You don't know how to have fun anymore."

Asshole.

"Fine. I'll show you how fun I am," I said, kicking off my boots.

"Woo-hoo," he hollered. "Nella's letting the old hair down."

I pulled my shirt over my head and pushed my jeans to the ground, careful to stay in the shadows for modesty's sake. "Shut up. Just shut up."

I gingerly walked toward the water, gasping at the squishy bottom of the pond. I'd forgotten all about that.

"Ugh. This is gross."

"Just jump in and start swimming. Then you don't have to feel the dead stuff on the bottom."

"What dead stuff?" I asked, getting ready to run back up on the shore.

"Just get in."

I swam to the middle of the pond and started to tread water, too. I had to say it was a gorgeous night with just enough moonlight to make the water glisten as our swimming sent ripples through it.

"Feels good, huh?" he asked.

Just then something brushed my foot. "Oh my god! What was that?" I screamed.

Jake laughed and swam away from me. "It was my foot, silly. You think the creature from the black lagoon is real or something? New York has really knocked your screws loose, Nella."

I floated onto my back, watching the water bead up on my body in the light. The night was silent except for the scream of crickets and the occasional bird that had not yet retired for the evening.

I spotted Jake on the other side of the pond and swam over to him.

He pushed his short hair back off his handsome

face. "You know, you were wrong about my being the same person I was in high school. You don't know what I've been doing with my life, other than the fact that I work in your dad's shop and I drive the same car."

He had a point.

And that had been a shitty thing to say.

"So what have you been doing?" I asked.

"Lots of things, like saving money for college. I have almost all that I need, so I don't have to work but part time for four years. I aced the SATs and now am in the process of applying."

Holy shit. He *had* been doing something with his life.

And I'd been totally out of line.

He continued. "You know my family didn't have the money to send me to college. So I'm getting there on my own. Your dad's been super supportive. He paid for my SAT prep course."

Dad did that?

Fuck. I'd been gone so long and there was so much I didn't know.

"That's… that's awesome, Jake. I'm impressed."

What a bitch I'd been. This guy's life had been pretty much an uphill battle and yet he'd been making things happen anyway.

I'd had all these opportunities and what had I done with them?

Become an expert at making ten-step coffee drinks.

I started swimming back to shore.

"Getting cold?" Jake asked, breast stroking next to me.

I nodded. "Maybe."

He swam ahead. "I'll tell you what. I have towels in the car. Let me grab them and I can hand you one as soon as you come out of the water. That way you won't get any colder."

Now I was really feeling badly for not being nicer. What the fuck was wrong with me?

He ran up to his car and returned with a towel wrapped around himself. He held the extra one open and turned away as I got out of the water.

"Okay. Got it," I said, shivering.

"C'mon. Grab your clothes," he said, leading the way back to his car.

Once there, he cranked up the heat and the chill disappeared as we dried off.

"Why won't you believe me that I told no one about our having sex way back when?" he asked.

"Well, if it wasn't you, then who did blab? I mean, who would have known?"

He looked out the driver side window, avoiding my gaze.

"I… I don't know. I mean, I'm not sure who it was," he said. "Hey, are you warming up?" he asked, taking my hand and rubbing it between his.

I started to pull away, but his touch felt so nice, and I remembered why I was so in love with him once.

But that was a long time ago.

And before I knew it, he'd pulled my hand to his lips and began to kiss my warming skin.

"That tickles," I laughed.

He stopped for a moment. "I know. I remember."

Shit. It was so strange to be with someone from the past, who knew me and everything about me—at one time in my life.

But I was a different person now. At least, I believed I was.

Was *he* different, as he claimed to be? I mean, how much did people change?

While I was tormenting myself with confusing thoughts, he leaned toward me and pushed the wet hair off my forehead. Then, taking hold of my chin, he turned my face toward his and kissed me like we'd never been apart.

This wasn't good. Not at all.

But I wasn't about to stop.

Against my better judgment, I fell into his arms, our lips and tongues exploring. And, not surprisingly, my towel fell open.

"You're so beautiful. More than ever, Nella," he breathed as he took my nipple in his mouth.

First, he ran his tongue over it, then closed his lips and tugged, sending a sweet pleasure/pain sensation shooting right to my core. I found my legs parting slightly as his free hand wandered over my thigh, as if to give him permission to meet me there.

I gasped as two of his fingers found my pussy and ran through my lips, teasing me by circling my clit with his thumb.

"God, Jake, that feels so nice," I whispered.

"A bit more skillful than the last time, I hope to god," he laughed.

Finally, he slipped a finger inside me and began to pump, keeping his thumb on my clit.

My whole body quivered with expectation, and with one last stroke, I bore down on his hand, convulsing in orgasm.

"Yeah, baby," he murmured. "Come for me. Let me feel your pussy tighten around my hand."

"Oh... oh, Jake. Yes," I whispered, struggling to catch my breath. "Just like that."

Okay. I was in trouble now. First Sebastian and then Jake. The only one left was Gus.

Not that I was going there with him.

I had to draw the line somewhere.

19

GUS MARTINS

"Morning, guys. Hey, where's Nella?"

Sebastian shrugged. Jake just looked away.

I knew it. Fucker had something up his sleeve.

"Looks like my friend Jake here has something he'd rather not share," I said in a sing-song voice.

He stretched himself up to his full height and approached me.

I bit my lip to avoid smiling. I guess what seemed funny was he needed to out-alpha me. But the truth was, my fighting days were behind me. They were what had landed me in prison, and I'd vowed never to lay a hand on anyone again.

"Hey, it's all good, man," I said, holding my hands up.

He wrinkled his brow. "I know. I'm just getting up to close the door."

Oh. Well. Shows what years in prison will do to a man's reflexes.

I wondered when the time would come that I'd no longer define life into the 'before' prison, and 'after' categories.

At some point, people around me would no longer see me as an ex-con first, and as a guy second. But when would I see myself that way?

Ever?

It haunted me.

"Nella's coming in a bit later this morning," Jake said. "Something about bringing her dad some stuff from the house."

Sebastian looked up from the work orders he was going through. "And you know this *how*?"

Jake shrugged. "I was with her last night."

There. There it was. Guess he'd already made his claim on the woman.

Kind of bummed me out.

I'd not had my chance. Not that she'd ever give me one. But I wouldn't have minded trying.

"I gotta confess, guys. I feel a little guilty, especially knowing you two are together," I looked right at Jake, "but she's one special lady. Smart, takes no shit, and good-looking as hell."

I looked down and shook my head. It was just as well. I had no business going after the boss's daughter, especially when she was in charge of things in his absence, and would just hightail it back to New York first chance she got, anyway.

But still.

Sure, there were a lot of women out there and it was easy to get a lay—especially for a burly guy like me. Women often had a fetish for my kind. Like it was their goal in life to fuck someone you wouldn't want to meet in a dark alley, and then brag to their friends about it. They all wanted one night with a guy who they'd never introduce to their parents. And I was okay with that.

They seldom wanted to see me again, and I felt the same way. I had no interest in tying myself down with a woman, at least at this stage of my life, so I was happy to fuck the pretty girls that came my way, make sure they were well satisfied, and then forget all about them.

Harsh, but that's life.

Half the time I didn't even ask their names, and the other half, I forgot as soon as they'd told me.

Kind of a fucked-up existence, but when you'd

been to prison, getting back to 'normal' took some work.

Had that time come?

Jake shook his head. "No, Gus. We're not together. I have no claim on her."

Now that was interesting.

"What do you mean?"

He tilted his head. "We were together last night, yes. But if you're interested, pursue it. Look, I'm getting ready to go back to school. Nella's an awesome woman, but my availability is going to be very limited."

Sebastian looked up from his paperwork. "That's cool of you, Jake."

He laughed. "Hey, same goes for you."

"What's that mean?" Sebastian asked.

Jake threw his hands out. "Dude. I've seen how you look at her. And I just may have seen you kissing her the other day…"

Sebastian's eyebrows rose.

Busted.

"Okay. Looks like we're all interested in the lovely Nella. Is that going to be a problem for us? I mean, we're a tight team. We work together well. Bud takes good care of us. I know none of us would want to fuck that up," he said.

"As far as I'm concerned, we can all date her," Jake said.

Damn. Jake and Sebastian were ballers. Where I came from, you didn't go near a woman another guy had been with. Even if they had nothing going on, he sort of had a claim on her. Stupid, I know. But that's how it was.

"Listen to you guys, all progressive and shit," I said.

Who knew?

"Gus, ask her out. It's fine," Sebastian said. "Sure, I like her. But I have no claim on her, just like Jake doesn't."

Well, I'd be damned. Of course I wasn't at all certain that the woman wanted a damn thing to do with me, especially with how I'd massively bungled my first impression, throwing all sorts of cheesy sexual innuendos her way.

That was the last time I'd pull something stupid like that. Lesson learned. You never knew who you were speaking to, and judging someone by the way they looked was just bad policy.

So, I figured I'd start by apologizing. Acknowledging my fuck up. I'd been staying out of Nella's line of fire, but that was a stupid way to go about things. I could bury my head in car engines for only so long. I'd eventually have to interact with her, and it would be best to do it on my own terms.

But most importantly, I needed this damn job. Employment opportunities for ex-cons were slim pickings, and I knew I was especially lucky to have landed this gig with a boss as supportive as Bud, and kick-ass coworkers like Sebastian and Jake. I couldn't blow this. No, I couldn't.

And I had to make Nella understand that.

She seemed like a reasonable woman, and if she were anything like her father, she'd understand where I was coming from. As it was, I was already almost out of a place to live.

Life after prison was full of fits and starts. I'd known that when they let me out. Some things worked out well and others did not.

All I could do was continue to move forward and do my best, which was exactly what I had in mind for Nella.

20

GUS MARTINS

"Gus," Sebastian said quietly, bending down over the VW engine I was working on, "there's a reporter in Nella's office. He's asking about you."

Those words hit me so hard I almost spilled all my tools, which would have been a fucking pain in the ass.

"Dammit," I growled, looking discreetly in the direction of the shop's office. Through the door, I could see some nosy-ass douchebag pressing Nella for dirt about me.

C'mon darlin'. Hook a guy up.

"Don't worry, man. She's a good girl. She'll cover for ya," he said.

I was sure Sebastian was right. But I was leaving nothing to chance.

"I'm going over there," I said.

But Sebastian put a hand on my arm. "Don't do it. Follow Nella's lead. If she thinks the guy is cool, she'll connect you two. But if he smells like trouble, she'll chase him off. Believe me. I know the woman," he said.

Christ, I was liking her more all the time.

But it wasn't easy to hang back and let Nella do my bidding. The fact that there was a reporter, whose desire for a good story took precedence over my privacy and well-being, made me blind with rage.

The sort of rage that got me in prison to begin with.

So I was going to keep my cool. As if there were a choice.

"Okay, Okay. "I'm just going to listen in. See exactly what the asshole is looking for."

Sebastian nodded, stepping aside. I crept over to the office's window, which opened into the shop, where I could listen just out of sight.

"Excuse me, how did you decide to pay us a visit here at Bryson's?" Nella asked stiffly.

The reporter chuckled. "Like I said, Miss Bryson, it's a matter of public record that your shop here is participating in the program to help ex-convicts get back on their feet. It's a great program and it's wonderful you are helping people."

I knew all that was public record. But that was probably news to Nella. Nevertheless, she didn't let that trip her up.

"Gotcha," she said. "Well, Gus isn't here right now. So, I'll show you out the door. But maybe before you come next time, you could call first to make sure he's in. I hate to see you waste your time coming all the way over here."

I heard her chair scrape the floor, and knew she was ushering him out. Or at least was trying to.

"If I could ask you one thing before you go…" she said.

"Sure. Anything," the reporter said hopefully.

"What are you hoping to accomplish by showing up here unannounced? Do you think that a man who was once in prison doesn't deserve the same privacy considerations everybody else does? What if he didn't want to talk? I mean, the man is trying to rebuild his life. Do you really think he wants to rehash everything with you for all your nosy readers to gossip about?"

Damn. I might just ask that woman to marry me.

And her words had the desired effect. "Well… um… Miss Bryson… it's just that we thought the, um, town would be interested in knowing how your business was helping Gus Martins. It could be good publicity for you."

Oh no. Nella was going to see through that in a second.

"Thanks for thinking of us," she said, and I heard the door squeak open. "We don't really need any publicity. My dad's shop has been here probably since before you were born. And I would bet—just guessing really—that our employee Gus Martins would rather not rehash what was probably the shittiest part of his life. So I'll ask you to please not return."

As they rounded the corner, I stepped into the storage room. When they'd passed, I leaned out to see the reporter hightail it to his car.

I was waiting for Nella when she returned to the office.

I was so in awe, I couldn't say anything for a moment.

"Gus," she said, "did you hear any of that?"

I nodded. She was as great a person as her father.

I finally got my voice back. "Thank you, Nella. Thank you for taking care of me back there. It was a really solid thing to do."

She smiled, and her bright red lips illuminated the room. "It was my pleasure. I can understand the paper wanting to do a story on the program that brought you to us, but I think their motives were more salacious than altruistic. Plus, we can't have our workers distracted, right?" she laughed.

I nodded. "True. We are pretty freaking busy and in fact, I'm gonna get back to that car—"

While nodding in agreement with me, Nella took a step back without looking behind her. Unfortunately, there was a pile of crap her father had left behind—one of many land mines in the office—and when her heel hit it, she began to stumble back.

Her eyes grew wide as her balance got away from her, and her arms waved as if to grab some sort of imaginary support.

But just as she started to go down, I caught her, and while it took a second for both of us to get her upright again, she was back on her feet in a matter of moments.

Right behind her, in her path should she have fallen, was a rusty, rickety old filing cabinet that had outlived its useful life, like a lot of Bud's crap. I had no doubt the monstrosity would have resulted in some nasty cuts and bruises had she collided with it, which she surely would have had I not been there.

"Whoa. Holy shit. Are you okay?" I asked.

We'd never been in such close proximity, and while I knew the normal thing to do would be to release her as soon as she was on solid ground, I continued holding her arms where I'd grabbed them to keep her upright.

And fuck if she didn't smell nice. Not overly perfumed like a lot of the chicks I met, but more subtle. Like simple lotion or one of those sorts of things women always seemed to like.

She looked up at me, expectantly, I supposed waiting for me to release her.

But I didn't.

Instead, I pulled her closer, almost in slow motion to give her plenty of time to protest. She turned her face to mine, and our lips met as if we'd been waiting forever for each other.

Well, at least I felt like I'd been waiting forever.

21

NELLA BRYSON

"Oh my god, Izzy, can you talk?"

The TV blared in the background with some sort of children's show, and I heard a couple of her kids yelling, and one crying.

"Oh sure, honey. Your timing is perfect. Although if this little one doesn't stop screaming, I may take her back to the store where I got her." She cackled loudly, and the baby calmed.

Before I jumped into the litany of my own problems, I checked in.

"Hey, how are you feeling? You must be a couple months out?" I asked.

She groaned. "Oh girl, and it's gonna be a long fucking couple of months. I am already as big as a house and keep peeing my pants." She laughed again.

And I did too. She hadn't changed a bit since we were kids, except now that she was pumping out babies as fast as she could.

"You'd think I'd learn to keep that goddamn husband of mine off me, but I can't resist the bastard."

I had no doubt her children were going to grow up to have filthy mouths just like she did. But their hearts would be as big, too.

"How is Rich, anyway?" I asked.

I heard the phone clatter the floor, followed by a loud, "Shit!"

"Sorry 'bout that, hon. I was juggling a kid on my hip."

Guess she got a lot of practice doing that.

"You know, Izzy, you can put the phone on speaker. That way you don't have to hold it to your ear."

I'd told her this before.

"Oh that's right. I keep forgetting. Pregnancy brain, I guess. So whatcha wantin' to talk about, hon?"

I took a deep breath. Where to start? I looked out

the office window and the guys were all busy working on cars.

"Well, you won't believe this, Izzy, but I have um… well, I have been with the guys."

She snorted. "I know you've been with guys. What, did you think I thought you were a virgin?"

Oh god.

"No, Izz. I mean, I've been with *the* guys. The guys at the shop."

Izzy didn't say anything for a moment, and then I heard a flurry of activity in the background. The TV clicked off, and she shooed the kids out of the family room.

"C'mon kids. Take your little sister upstairs and put her down for her nap. Both of you. Now. I need to have a talk with Aunt Nella."

The protests faded as Izzy herded them up the stairs and out of earshot.

"Are you serious?" she said in a near-whisper. "Tell me everything. Please. This is so exciting I'm shaking."

"So, I've kissed Sebastian, and Gus, the new guy."

She gasped. "Isn't the new guy an ex-con? Is that what I heard?"

"Yes, he is—"

"Oh my god. You kissed an ex-con. Are you gonna fuck him?" she asked.

For Christ's sake.

"Izzy, would you please just listen? Let me tell my story before you make it all complicated. And confusing."

I checked again to make sure the guys were busy with cars. The last thing I needed was for them to hear me agonizing over them.

"Okay," she said quietly. "Continue."

"Okay. So like I said, I've kissed both Seb and Gus. But…" I hesitated, wondering if she was going to give me the lecture to end all lectures, "I've done a little more than just kiss Jake."

"Wow," she breathed.

"Yeah, so I'm a fucking idiot, messing around with each of my dad's employees, who, while Dad's out, are sort of *my* employees.

"Nella, I gotta tell you—"

I held my breath, waiting for the scolding.

"—that is one of the hottest fucking things I've ever heard."

Um, what?

"It is not *hot*, Izzy. It is stupid. Reckless. Irresponsible. And if my dad finds out, he'll fire all three of them and kick my ass, too."

Izzy went quiet on me again.

"Hey, Izz. You there?"

"Mmmm-hmmm," she said. "I gotta tell ya, Nell,

no matter what you say, I think this is hot. It makes me kind of wish I'd waited to get married so I could have some crazy experiences like this."

"Are you kidding?" I asked, watching the guys gather for a coffee break. "Shit. I gotta go. But Izz—do you think I'm crazy? Playing with fire?"

"Honey, playing with fire is completely under-rated. In fact, I think you should play with *more* fire. And if you get burned every now and then, so be it. You'll survive."

Easy for her to say.

22

NELLA BRYSON

The guys wandered to my office.

"Hey, Nella, how about an afternoon coffee?" Jake asked.

His expression gave away nothing. If he'd kept his mouth shut, no one would know we'd been together the other night.

And what a night it was. He hadn't been kidding when he'd said that over the years he'd acquired some 'skills,' and those skills had nearly driven me out of my mind. Later, I'd lain awake almost all night long thinking about the way he'd stroked me.

"Um, yeah, sure. I'll take a coffee." I reached for my wallet, but he held his hand up.

"I got it, babe—I mean Nella."

He turned about a thousand shades of red, and the other guys snickered.

Okay. Guess there weren't many secrets in the place. If that's the way it was, then so be it.

The guys left and I buried myself again in the cryptic system my dad had set up for payroll. Why he hadn't hired one of those companies to take care of it was beyond me. Figuring out taxes and shit was about the most mind-boggling boring job I'd ever tackled and on top of that, I knew the chances of my making a mistake were pretty high.

So I decided to call him.

"Bella Nella!" he exclaimed when he answered on the first ring. "Are you doing right by me down there at the shop, honey?"

Rubbing my eyes, I groaned. "Dad, I'm stuck on this payroll stuff. It's so complicated. Can I bring it to you and you'll help me?"

I still needed to give him that card from my mother.

"Sure, darlin', but, um, not right now. I'm kind of…busy."

Busy? How can you be busy in rehab with a shattered leg? I'd heard they had arts and crafts, but that wasn't my dad's jam.

Neither had meditation been, either…

"What do you mean, busy?" I asked.

"Well, sweetie, Dakini is here and we were about to start a meditation after she showed me a little chair yoga. Although, I need something more like bed yoga," he chuckled as Dakini giggled in the background.

Oh my god. They were a thing. I should have known her visit and all their Namaste bullshit were not a one-off. How the hell old was she, anyway?

Not much older than I, I was sure of that. And she was into my dad?

Ewww.

But if I thought that was 'ewww,' I hadn't heard the best part.

"Sweetie, if we could make it tomorrow, maybe after lunch time or something, that would be great. You see, Dakini and I have put in for what we call a 'conjugal visit,'" he said.

More giggling.

"Wha… what the hell is that, Dad?"

And then it occurred to me.

"Oh god, never mind, Dad, I don't want to know. You and Dakini have fun and call me back when you are free."

"Okay, honey, thanks for understanding. I really need this. Dakini has brought so much healing to my life. I don't want to lose my momentum. *We* don't want to lose *our* momentum."

Just when the thought of Dad with the hot yoga teacher couldn't get any grosser, I heard them start to kiss.

While on the phone with me.

No. That was just too much.

I swiped my phone closed, trying to also swipe my mind clean of Dad and Dakini's 'conjugal' visits.

Dad's rehab place permitted that shit?

Once again, I buried my head in my hands. I wanted to take all the stupid paperwork before me and just throw it in the trash. But if I did that, the guys wouldn't get paid. And that would not be cool.

"Hey, you got a headache or something?" Sebastian asked as he pushed open my door, startling me.

"Oh. No. I mean, well, sort of. This payroll stuff is a headache."

He walked behind me and looked over my shoulder. "Oh. Geez. Wish I could help you with that, but it's way beyond my pay grade."

"It's beyond my pay grade, too," I said, stretching my neck. "What did you bring back? That doesn't look like coffee."

He held up a plain paper bag, and pulled out two beers. "I figured you could use one of these."

"Gimme, gimme." I reached my hand out like a starving animal. "Will this make the pain of my day go away?"

He took the seat opposite my desk. "If you drink enough of them, you won't feel a goddamn brick fall on your foot. But I don't recommend that."

I rolled my shoulders and stretched again, hoping the stiffness would leave my body, but knowing I was probably stuck with it.

"Here. Let me help you with that," Sebastian said, setting down his beer and walking behind my chair.

He brushed my hair aside and laid his giant hands on my shoulders. With his thumbs on my neck, he started to knead.

Slowly.

And like a happy puppy, my eyes fell closed as his touch washed over me. His fingers dug into the tight muscles and fascia causing my discomfort, and even though it would have taken an hour of such massaging to knock it entirely out of my system, the warmth of his strong hands instantly helped me relax.

The struggles of doing payroll suddenly didn't seem so overwhelming.

And neither did the fact that his touch was

causing my breath to come in small gasps and my head to fall forward, limp on my neck.

Shit. I was in trouble now.

And even more so when his lips brushed the back of my neck.

A moment more of this and I knew there was no turning back.

"God, Seb, that feels so nice," I purred, rolling my head around to give him more access to my sensitive flesh.

"Excellent, baby. I want you to feel good," he whispered, his lips grazing my ear.

Everything in my brain was screaming *stop*. But the thought quickly lost meaning when he reached over my shoulder and wrapped his fingers around my erect nipple.

"Ahhhh," I moaned.

Slipping his hand down my shirt and bra, he pinched harder.

It was like the pain-pleasure sensation had a direct line to my core, which burst into an ache I knew would have to be dealt with soon.

Very soon.

I clamped one hand over Sebastian's to increase the pressure, and reached the other overhead to touch him when my office door flew open, startling the shit out of me.

"Well. What do we have here?" Gus asked, unfazed.

Interesting reaction.

If I wasn't mistaken, a big erection was already tenting Gus's pants.

Good god. That guy wasted no time.

And I wasn't mistaken. With a wicked grin, Gus ran his open palm down his crotch and when he pulled it away, revealed the outline of the biggest cock I'd ever seen.

I wanted to ask him to go, but I also wanted to ask him to stay.

But I did neither, hoping he and Sebastian would make the decision.

And they did.

23

SEBASTIAN GREER

Well, fuck a duck.

Playtime was over before it even got started.

Or was it?

On one hand, I wanted to belt the fucking smile off Gus's face for cock-blocking me. I mean, Nella and I were seriously getting into it and any fool would know to leave us the hell alone so we could do our thing.

He had a lot of nerve to blow in and potentially put a stop to our little party. After all, it wasn't exactly on the up-and-up that I was messing around with the boss's daughter. While there was no doubting our attraction to each other, the actual real-life connection was fragile at best.

She could kick me out at any moment. Tell me to get the hell off her and out of her office.

Hell, if she really wanted to make my life difficult, she could even say I'd pushed myself on her against her will. It would be a lie, but you never knew what a person would do when under pressure.

On the other hand, there was no doubt she was Bud's daughter, and I knew she didn't have it in her to screw anyone over.

And yet, we'd been caught red-handed by Gus, who was just waiting for an invitation to join the party.

Actually, he wasn't really waiting. He'd already invited himself. I had to hand it to the man—he certainly had balls.

I didn't mind if he stuck around. The shop was closed and Jake had left ages ago to go home to study or something. Gus had just locked the garage doors, so there was no chance of anyone else coming in.

Not that we needed anyone else. Three was plenty, especially for a girl like Nella who, I suspected, had little experience with 'group' activities.

There was only one way to find out how she felt about the situation before her.

Gauge her reaction.

She could kick us both the hell out.

She could tell Gus to hit the road since she and I had already started our fun times.

Or—she could welcome him and the three of us could see how things unfolded.

For a moment, both Gus and I figuratively held our breath, waiting to see what she'd do. I still had a hand down her shirt, and Gus, stroking himself, was slowly making his way in our direction.

Since she hadn't pulled the plug on anything, I got back to kissing her neck and playing with her nipple.

"Looks like we have someone else joining the party, baby," I whispered in her ear.

I glanced at Gus, who came around her desk on the opposite side of where I stood. He took her hand, and placed it right on his dick.

Damn. That guy didn't mess around.

And as he did, I reached for Nella's other nipple. I pulled them both as she caressed Gus, her excitement clear with her eager strokes.

Gus rocked himself into her slightly, doing nothing more than following her lead. And his patience paid off.

With two hungry hands, she attacked his belt and fly, releasing him through a tangle of shirt tails and boxer shorts. To be honest, I had no interest in looking at another guy's package, but the eagerness she displayed when she had him in her hands, and then licked his cockhead, was almost enough to make me explode in my pants.

"You cool with this, Seb?" Gus asked.

"Fuck yeah. As long as Nella is."

Her eyes widened, and she nodded enthusiastically.

"You do stuff like this in the big city, baby?" Gus asked, smiling.

She stopped licking him for a moment. "Actually, no." She laughed. "Never. Who knew my first time in a, um… group activity would be here in my hometown in my dad's shop?"

I sure as hell had never anticipated this.

"Hey, you're sure your dad's laid up right? Like, he's not gonna waltz right in here to sign checks or something, is he?" Gus asked.

She laughed. "He's pretty much stuck where he is. I wouldn't worry about him. We're safe."

"Last I saw of him, that poor man won't be mobile for quite a while. He's not going to come blasting in here for a long time," I added.

Then Nella looked between the two of us, her

heavy-lidded, glittery blue eyes reminding me of a languid feline. "So what about you, Gus, you a pro at this stuff?"

She giggled.

"Baby, I was in the slammer for ten years, so I'm a bit rusty on all my life skills. But I'd like to think I can get by."

They both looked in my direction. "Seb?"

"I ain't saying anything to incriminate myself." I laughed.

I'd never, in all the years I'd spent at Bryson's Garage, from the time I was barely old enough to hold a wrench, to the first time Bud had shown me how to do an engine replacement, imagined I'd be messing around in his office. On one hand, I suspect he'd be glad for me. He knew the guys working for him were young men and that we had a lot of wild oats to sow. But on the other, if he were aware we were with his daughter—well, that might not be too pretty.

While all this talk was going on, Gus and I had lifted Nella from her chair. I pulled her shirt off over her head, and Gus had lowered her jeans, leaving her in nothing but a lacy thong and matching bra. He gently laid her back on the desk and parted her legs.

Pushing aside the crotch of her panties, he dove between her legs with an appetite that caused her to arch her back and call out, reaching for his head to pull him down closer.

Fuck me. She was sexier than I'd even imagined.

I slipped her bra straps down her arms to get to her ripe tits, and in moments, I had her nipples hard and wet from my attentions. Gus continued eating her pussy, one hand stroking himself at the same time.

I moved from Nella's tits to her luscious lips, and her mouth fell open, accepting my exploring tongue, the vibrations of her moans echoing through me.

"Give me your cock, Seb," she muttered, reaching for my fly.

In moments, I was banging against the back of her throat. She'd lifted her head and grabbed the cheeks of my ass to pull me in. I had to say it was one of the hottest fucking things I'd ever experienced. Gus was pumping her pussy with two fingers while his mouth worked her clit, and she was sucking me with a pleasure that brought me close to exploding.

But I wasn't ready yet. None of us were.

She released me for a moment. "Gus, get a condom."

"Gotcha, baby," he said, reaching into the back pocket of his jeans.

While Gus sheathed himself, I lifted Nella off the

desk where she'd been lying, and turned her to bend over the desk. While Gus inched her legs apart, I crawled up on the desk to get my cock back in her mouth.

With her face in my lap and Gus behind her, we tagged teamed the lovely Nella.

Gus thrust into her pussy, which pushed her deeper onto my cock. I wove my fingers into her silky black hair and held her on me, rocking my hips for more depth as she gagged on my erection.

When I finally released her, she coughed and gasped for breath, her eyes watering. But she smiled up at me and while being pounded from behind, closed her eyes, her mouth slightly open, and cried out as she came.

"C'mon, baby," Gus said, "come for me. Come for me and Seb."

I lowered her head on my cock just in time to shoot my load. She gobbled my cum hungrily, her eyes still watering from my banging her mouth.

Gus's groans had been building, and at last he exploded in a fury that nearly pushed Nella off the desk and across the room.

Luckily I was there to catch her.

"Oh god, Gus, fuck me, please fuck me like that," she screamed, gripping my hand so hard I thought she might break it.

Later, she looked up from the desk, first at me and then around to Gus and smiled, her head dropping in exhaustion.

Jesus, I was in trouble.

We all were.

24

SEBASTIAN GREER

AFTER CATCHING OUR BREATH, GUS AND I GUIDED Nella over to the sofa in the office. I sat at one end and he at the other, and we lay Nella between us with her head in my lap and her feet in his.

She looked up at me while I stroked her hair, her eye makeup slightly smudged, her lipstick completely kissed off, looking more beautiful than I'd ever seen her.

"Yikes," Nella breathed, "it's getting late. And yet, I hate to move."

"Me too, baby," I said, smiling down on her.

How the fuck did I get so lucky?

"What time is it?" Gus asked.

"Seven-ish," Nella said, pointing at the wall clock.

I groaned. "Shit. I told my mother I'd take her grocery shopping."

Nella popped her head up. "Oh my god. How is your mother? I've been so wrapped up with myself I haven't even asked."

Nella knew my life story about as well as anyone. "Well, you probably know she left my bastard father years ago. But money is tight for her and she doesn't like to accept help. So I do what I can and hope she doesn't notice. Like when we go grocery shopping, I'll get a bunch of stuff, pretending it's for me, and then sneak it in and put it away in her kitchen."

Nella squeezed my hand. "You're a good guy, Seb."

Then, she looked down at the other end of the sofa. "What about you, Gus? Everything coming together?"

He winced. "Well, I've hit another rough patch," he said. "My landlady just found out I'm an ex-con and wants me the hell out. It's not easy for a guy like me to find a place to live, and on top of it, I now have two cats."

"You have cats?" Nella asked incredulously.

Gus laughed. "Yes, I have cats. In fact, I need to get home to feed them. They're greedy little beasts."

Nella sat up on the sofa, all excited. "Gus, I may be able to help you out. Why don't you stay here in the shop for a while? This sofa pulls out, and you know there's a shower in the locker room."

"You know, Jake mentioned something about that to me," he said.

Nela turned to me. "What do you think, Seb? You think that would be okay?"

She was just like her dad, always looking for ways to help people out.

"It's up to you, beautiful. My only stipulation would be that Gus not jerk off all over the place. I don't want my workplace to be all sticky and shit."

He dropped his head back on the sofa and laughed. "You got me there, brother. I plan to spill my seed on every surface of this place. In fact, I already have, right where you're sitting."

I jumped to my feet. "That is fucking nasty, dude. Ugh. I think I'm gonna barf."

I looked at Nella who was laughing so hard she was shaking. "You guys..."

I tossed Nella her clothes and began pulling on my own. "Nell, you wanna come with me, to take Mom to the store? She'd probably love to see you."

She nodded. "That sounds awesome. And then maybe tomorrow figure out when Gus moves in?"

"Damn, Nella, that's very generous of you."

"I'm excited to have a couple *shop cats*."

"Well, I'm excited to have a *shop babe*," I said, taking Nella's hand and leading her to my car.

25

NELLA BRYSON

"Honey, I hear you're really doing a bang-up job down at the shop."

Oh shit. What had my dad heard?

That I'd slept with all the employees, whom I was now supposed to be managing? That I'd accepted bad checks? Or how about that I'd messed up the payroll so badly I'd just paid the guys out of petty cash, which, by the way, was way too much cash to keep sitting around the office.

Banks exist for a reason, Dad.

There were so many things to discuss with him that I'd actually made a list. So, I grabbed the guest chair next to his bed, and made myself at home with the notebook I pulled out of my bag.

But not before noticing the soft pashmina shawl someone had left behind, which smelled an awful lot like the yoga teacher.

The one my dad was planning 'conjugal' visits with.

The taste of vomit bubbled up in my throat, and I swigged from the water bottle I'd brought from home.

It's not that she wasn't a nice person. In fact she was very nice. Just that morning, when I was pulling out of the driveway to come see Dad, she'd flagged me down with a yam muffin.

That's right. A *yam* muffin.

"It's paleo," she beamed. "Hey, will you bring this one along to your father, Nella? I won't be able to come by until later today and I don't want him subsisting on that over processed facility food."

At least I knew Dad wouldn't starve.

She held up a finger before I took off. "Say, Nella, I wanted to offer you some yoga classes. At my studio."

Now she was talking.

"That's really nice of you, Dakini," I said, forcing myself to take a bite of the hideous, dry muffin she'd given me.

"You know, Nella, I've been wanting to talk to you about something else."

I wanted to say I was all ears, but I was trying not to choke on the muffin.

So I just nodded.

"Your father, Bud, is a good man," she said with a very serious face. "And we've become very close. I'll never forget the day I heard him fall from the ladder. I was changing out of my yoga clothes—I'd just gotten home from the studio—and I heard this loud *crash*. I threw on my robe and ran out to find your father in complete agony, writhing on the ground in great pain."

I wanted to say *served him right*, but I wasn't that mean.

"I went with him to the hospital, and that's when it all started."

Okay, if that's what she wanted to believe. She didn't need to know Dad had been watching her for god knew how long.

I wouldn't rat my own father out, but I wondered if I should tell her about the other men in the neighborhood and their spying.

Actually, I couldn't see any good coming from it, so I decided not to. Besides, I had to get going.

And I didn't want dad's yam muffin to get any drier than it already was.

"Thanks for looking out for my dad, Dakini. It's very kind of you."

She tilted her head and smiled.

I didn't get a *Namaste* this time.

I handed Dad the pashmina I'd almost sat on, which most certainly belonged to Dakini. "Hey, someone left this behind."

One eyebrow rose and he broke into a smile. He brought it up to his nose for a deep inhale, and sighed, stuffing it under his pillow.

Who had kidnapped my father? Because the man in front of me couldn't possibly be him.

"What do you mean I'm doing a *bang-up* job? Who told you that?" I asked, holding my breath.

This could be very good news—or very bad news.

"Oh, Seb was by earlier this morning. Told me you had everything under control."

Yeah, I bet he'd said that.

"He said you were whipping the place into shape and somehow making sense of my disorganization." He slapped his good leg and laughed.

Glad he thought it was so funny.

"So… Seb came by this morning? But it's a Saturday, and his day off."

Dad threw his hands up. "What can I say? The guys love me."

Yeah well, they seemed a little fond of me, too. But I kept that to myself.

"What else did he say?" I squeaked.

He shrugged. "Just that things were working out nicely. But I'm glad you came by today for another reason."

"What's that Dad?"

He pushed himself up in bed, like he had an important point to make.

"I want to thank you. Words can't describe the gratitude I have for your coming home to take over things while I convalesce. Your brother... well, let's not go there. But I've always known you'd be there for me if I needed you, and you were. Your mother would be so proud of you."

Well shit. He had to go and mention Mom.

My eyes watered and Dad's face got blurry.

"I know, honey. I miss her too," he said.

There was so much I wanted to ask, that I'd never thought to before.

How had it been for him, to lose his wife when he had teenage kids? Had it been so painful that he'd been compelled to hold onto all her things in order to keep any bit of her that he could, alive?

Even her perfume bottles still sat on her dresser —surrounded by dust, naturally—after all these years having turned into nothing more than nostril-burning alcohol.

"Hello, Mr. Bryson. Am I interrupting anything?"

We both whipped our heads to see a small man with glasses in a black polo shirt and khaki pants.

His name badge read Alan.

"Oh, hey. Come on in. This is my daughter, Nella. Sweetie, this is my PT—short for physical therapist."

Alan extended his hand. "I… I can come back if you need some more time," he said, looking between the two of us.

I shook my head. "No, no, that's fine. I was getting ready to head out, anyway. Say, Alan, how much longer do you think my father needs to be in here?"

Cocking his head, he rubbed his chin, staring at the mess that was my dad's leg. "I'd say… another two to three. But that's a guess."

"Two or three? Weeks?" I asked.

That wasn't so bad. I could get the shop organized and introduce some new business practices, leaving dad in good shape. He'd hit the ground running when he got back to work.

But Alan laughed. At me. "No, Miss Bryson. Not two to three weeks. Two to three *months*."

I gripped the seat of my chair as the news sank in

that Dad would be out of commission for a *long* fucking time.

This time I kept my big mouth shut instead of protesting the news, remembering how my big mouth got me kicked out of the last place Dad had been in.

"Seriously?" I peeped, my voice cracking.

I swallowed hard to lower my voice back to a normal range, and cleared my throat for good measure. "Two… two to three *months*, you say, Alan?"

Dad crossed his arms and nodded, resigned to the news. Why should he worry? He had me to run the business and was being fawned over by a sexy yoga instructor. With whom he could have 'conjugal' visits.

"Your dad's not exactly Wolverine, you know, with crazy mutant healing factors."

He smiled, pleased with his reference to popular culture.

But even without it, I got the picture.

Shit, shit, shit, shit.

Yeah, I was having a nice time being in town, reconnecting with the old gang, working in the garage, and even… ahem, spending 'time' with the guys. But I had a life to live back in New York. Even though I'd lost my job and place to live and my dick-head brother wouldn't call me back.

"Last I checked," Alan continued, "your father is not going to regenerate bone."

The two men looked at each other and guffawed like old buddies.

Fucked. That's what I was.

And not just literally.

26

NELLA BRYSON

I pulled Dad's car to the curb and ran-walked to the bar. It might only have been two p.m., but I needed a drink and I needed it right away.

Unfortunately for me, the bar was not open. In fact, the sign on the door read, in large mocking letters, *Open at 5.*

Dammit.

I looked across the street to the diner, where I spotted Izzy working behind the counter. This was actually way better than the bar. I needed to see my girl.

I slunk in and took a seat at a counter stool. Izzy spotted me immediately.

"Darlin'. Good to see ya," she said, wiping down the spot in front of me.

"I didn't think you were still working, Izz," I said, watching her waddle in an apron clearly not meant for a pregnant woman.

"Oh, I like to work up till the very last minute the baby comes. It's the last time I get away from the kids for a while," she said, cracking herself up. "The hubs is home with them and is probably hating life right about now."

She babbled on a bit about the family and her pregnancy, and how she was trying to get all the sex she could right now because when the baby came, it would be 'dry dock city' for at least a few weeks, and she'd for sure be too tired to give head.

I guess when you'd had as many kids as she had, you knew to plan for these things.

But in the middle of telling me about toilet training kid number three, she stopped, leaning over the counter toward me.

"Whoa. Wait a minute. I can see this is not a purely social visit. What's going on?"

I sighed long and loud.

Yeah, it was pity party time.

"Holy crap," she exclaimed, holding up one

finger, "I know what this is. It's a double chocolate milkshake sort of day, isn't it? Tell me I'm right, I can see it written all over your face. I *know* you, girlfriend. You can't pull anything over on me."

Looking down at my chipped manicure, I nodded.

When she returned with the icy concoction, I drew a hard sip through the straw and closed my eyes. As the cold slipped down my throat, my spirits lifted a little.

"Holy shit, Izz. This is pure heaven."

She slapped her hand on the counter. "I know, right. That's why I made myself one too!" she tapped her cup against mine like a toast.

"Okay, now that you have your chocolate medicine, spill. I need something to dream about while I'm up to my nose in baby diapers. You know I'm living vicariously through you. Right?"

"What? Why?"

She rolled her eyes. "Silly. I love my life, but, girl, you are doing all the things I never got to. You know, living in the big city, dressing like a rocker chick, and fucking all the hot guys you want."

Thank god the diner was empty except for an old dude in the corner who'd dozed off.

"It's not all roses, Izz, let me tell you."

She shrugged. "Okay. Tell me."

"To begin with, Dad's going to be in rehab for a long time. Like *months* long time."

She gave me her best 'duh' look. "What did you expect?"

I looked out the diner window at nothing in particular. "I don't know. I mean, I guess I thought he'd be fine in a week or two and I'd be back in New York. Guess I'm not that good with expectations. Like when we were in high school. I never expected to sleep with Jake and then for it to get all over school."

The corner of her mouth turned up in a snarl. "Seriously. His sister Louise is still just as big a bitch as she was in high school. Thank god she doesn't come in here anymore. I couldn't stand looking at her."

"What? What do you mean?"

She frowned. "Okay. You've got to know. After all these years."

"Know *what*?"

"That she was the one who spread it all over the school that you'd had sex with Jake. Are you only just now learning this?"

"Um, *yeah*. And why did you never tell me this before? All this time I thought it was Jake who opened his big mouth and bragged to his friends."

"Nella, back when it happened, you didn't want

to talk about it. I tried to tell you and you shut me down. But I would have sworn you'd have learned it by now. Yeah, Jake's horrible older sister trashed you up and down."

Suddenly, my chocolate shake didn't taste so great, and in fact, I felt like a lump of it was stuck right in the middle of my chest.

"Water?" I croaked.

Izzy hustled as fast as her pregnant body would let her, and returned with a tumbler that I consumed in one long gulp.

"You okay?" she asked.

No. I wasn't okay. I wasn't okay when I came in, and now I was even less okay.

I shook my head, the lump in my chest becoming more painful.

"All these years, Izz, I thought… well, guess I'm glad I slept with him, then."

She laughed. "Yeah, well that was a long time ago—"

I held my hand up to stop her. "No, I slept with him just the other night."

Her eyes widened and her jaw dropped. "You… but you also slept with the other guys at the shop, right?"

A smile crept across her face. "Holy shit, girl. You're fucking everyone. You know how hot that is?"

"I... I... I'm not so sure about that. And now I feel like total shit for blaming Jake all these years for the rumors."

I pushed my shake away. I'd had enough.

"Izz, I even brought up the whole high school thing the other day with Jake, and he didn't say a thing about his sister. Why would he cover for her? Does he not know?"

Izzy pressed her lips together. "Oh he knows. Everyone knows it was Louise."

"Then why didn't he say anything?"

She took a sip of what was left of my shake. "You'll have to ask him yourself."

27

JAKE PARKER

"Why didn't you ever tell me?"

I looked up from the transmission I was elbows deep in.

Gus and Sebastian looked our way, then quickly buried their heads under the car hoods where they were working, pretending to mind their own business.

Yeah, right.

"What are you talking about?" I asked.

"You know perfectly well what I'm talking about."

"Maybe we should speak in private?" I suggested.

Nella turned on her heel and stomped toward the office, assuming I'd be right behind her.

And she was right. But dammit, I hated being interrupted when I was working on a transmission. They were fucking complicated.

She should know that.

Nella had propped her butt up on her desk when I joined her, so I grabbed a seat on the sofa, right next to the door.

In case I needed to make a fast escape. She looked like she might be throwing a big, heavy stapler at my head at any moment.

"You never told me. All these years you let me think it was you."

Oh. That. Yeah. The chickens were coming home to roost. I always knew it would eventually happen.

"You are right," I said.

"Was it really your sister? Louise?"

I nodded slowly, avoiding her gaze. I'd agonized over this for so long.

"I… I didn't want anyone to know. Louise always had… so many problems. I didn't want to make them worse by giving you a reason to hate her. I didn't want *anyone* to hate her, and I knew they would. So I just let you hate me. And anyone else who felt inclined."

"Until the truth came out."

I nodded. In the end, all the covering for my sister had been for naught.

Confusion crossed Nella's face. "I guess I understand that. But Louise was always so nasty to you. And me. Why protect her?"

"She was jealous of you, Nella. So jealous."

"What? Of *me?*"

"You were pretty, popular, had a cool older brother who, by the way, wanted nothing to do with her even though she had a huge crush on him. You had a job working for your dad, you were going to college, you were going *places*... you just had everything she didn't."

She started pacing the small office, then turned to me. "You... you thought all those things of me?"

I'd left out *beautiful.* I didn't want to sound superficial.

"Nella, c'mon. Take a look at yourself. You had the balls to leave town. You freaking moved to New York. How many people in this town do you think have ever even *been* to New York?"

She took a seat next to me on the sofa. "I'm... really flattered. Thank you, Jake. And I'm sorry I never knew it was Louise who blabbed. How did she find out?"

I'd always wondered that myself.

"I supposed she figured it out when we were out

all night. It wasn't hard to guess if you were looking for it, you know, evidence of two kids sneaking off and having sex. But... there's something else I wanted to talk to you about, now that we're alone."

She gave me a smirk.

And damn if it wasn't fucking adorable.

"Oh. You mean about the other night? You know, I've been meaning to tell you it was much better than the last time," she giggled.

Gee thanks. The last time was almost ten freaking years ago.

"In fact," she said, flopping back on the sofa, "I think I'll give you a solid nine for your performance. That's a big improvement, you know. You should be proud."

I fake-frowned at her, but let her continue having her fun. I figured she deserved it.

She smacked her leg. "In fact, you know what I could do? How 'bout I write you a Yelp review!"

"Okay, enough," I said, laughing as I started to pull her over my lap.

"No, no," she protested, giggling.

I looked out the office window and saw Gus smiling and shaking his head.

Now she was fully face down on my lap, squirming and laughing.

"If you could be quiet for just a minute, I'll tell

you what's on my mind. But if you continue to misbehave, I will be forced to take action."

I smoothed my hand over her ass to make my point.

"Okay. Okay," she said, finally holding still.

"I think it's really nice how you're helping out Gus. He's a good guy. A really good guy. He fell into a bad situation, and deserves help getting out of it. So, thank you. You won't regret letting him move into the shop."

Seriously. If nothing else, he'd be an excellent security guard. Not that there was much of a problem with that sort of thing in town, but with Gus on site, no one would ever dare come around.

"Hey. Did I hear someone say my name?"

We both looked up to see Gus had popped his head in the door.

"Oh, hey. Yeah, I was just telling Nella what an asshole you were. You know, the usual."

Gus smiled and flipped me off. "And Nella, why are you hanging over Jake's lap? Is this spanking time or something?"

She squirmed in my grip, but at the same time, something in her breathing changed and her cheeks flushed as she looked at Gus's cock.

Jesus. The guy was already hard.

And hell if that hadn't turned on our dirty girl.

"Why yes, Gus, Nella is in need of a spanking. For so many reasons."

Laughing, she tried to escape. "You're so full of crap. Tell me one thing I've done to warrant a spanking."

Gus pulled up a chair and also started rubbing a hand over her ass.

"Well, Nella," I said, "you did forget to put milk in my coffee the other day."

"Oh god," Gus said. "That's a serious offense."

"Arrrgghhh," she screamed, trying to twist out of our restraint. "Okay. Tell me something else I've done."

I looked at Gus.

"Nella," he said softly, "you come in here every day looking so fucking beautiful you leave me with a hard on half the day. You know how many times I've had to go to the men's room to jerk myself off?"

She reached out to smack him, but hilariously missed. "That's gross. Oh my god, Gus. Jerking off at work. Who does that!"

Gus and I looked at each other. Our girl had so much to learn.

"Everybody does that, Nella," I said.

By now her arms were flailing. So Gus and I did the only thing we could. Placed them behind her back and held them together at the wrist.

"Ugh. You guys are gross. People most certainly do *not* masturbate at work."

Just then Sebastian stuck his head in the office. "Hey, kids, have fun. I'm taking off for the day."

"Seb, help me," Nella screamed, laughing.

"Sorry, baby, you're on your own," he called over his shoulder just before the door slammed behind him.

"C'mon guys. Let me up. I'll do anything," she squealed.

Those words were like music to our ears.

We released Nella, who shook herself out with a great deal of indignation.

"You gotta do what we ask now," Gus said.

Holy shit. I knew exactly where he was going with this.

"Yeah, yeah," she said.

"Since you are under the impression that *nobody* masturbates at work, we figured we'd prove you wrong. Starting with you."

She looked between the two of us, her brow furrowed.

Displaying the cutest little wrinkles.

"You guys are super funny. Ha ha ha ha."

She rolled her eyes and crossed her arms.

"Well, I do think we are funny guys. But we're serious at the moment," I said.

Gus got up from his chair, and indicated that Nella should take a seat.

"Okay. Here I am," she said, throwing her arms up in the air.

Gus took a seat on the sofa next to me, not even hiding the couple strokes he had for his cock.

The guy was such a baller. Totally cracked me up.

"Put your hand down your pants, Nella," he said.

"What? No."

He looked at me. "Guess we need to put her back over your knee, then."

I jumped to my feet and took a couple steps toward her.

But she stopped me by holding her hands up. "Okay. Jesus."

I sat back down to watch her slide her hand down into her jeans.

"That's what I'm talking about," Gus said. "How's it feel, baby?"

She nodded. "Nice."

"Now rub that clit. I want to see it on your face," he said.

After a minute or two, her eyelids got heavy, and she moistened her lips.

"Yeah," I said quietly. "Just like that, darlin'."

Out of the corner of my eye I could see that Gus

had whipped out his dick, and the longer Nella looked at it, the harder she stroked herself.

"Now pop a finger inside. Yeah, deep like that," I said.

"Now pull it out and taste it."

Gazing directly at me, she withdrew her hand and brought her finger up to her mouth, slowly slipping it between her lips, her eyes falling closed.

Well, fuck me. I didn't think I'd ever been as hard, and if I didn't have a little relief soon, I was going to lose my mind.

"Taste good?" I asked.

Although I knew the answer.

She nodded, continuing to suck.

"Do you think you could suck my cock like that?" I asked.

She nodded again.

"Okay. Come over here then. Gus is going to eat your pussy while you taste my dick."

Gus chuckled. "Fuck yeah, my man."

Nella sauntered over to the two of us, opening her blue jeans, and slipping them past her hips. She stepped out of one leg, following with her lacy panties.

I knew she was excited, but didn't know how fucking much until I caught the scent of her pretty pussy as Gus sat her on the sofa and parted her legs.

I caught a glimpse of her swollen pussy lips before Gus knelt before her and buried his face.

"Ohhhh," she moaned and Gus got to work.

But she wouldn't be able to moan for long, because her mouth was about to be full of my dick.

I stepped up onto the sofa and stood next to Nella, positioning myself right at her mouth. I leaned in to rub my precum on her lips, which she licked off like a kitten getting its first milk. Then, she opened her mouth and took me deep.

Jesus, this woman was goddamn sexy. There she was, sprawled out for Gus, who was making grunting noises as he devoured her pussy, and she was still eager to take my cock until it hit the back of her throat.

I held her head until she made gagging noises, and when I released her, she gasped for air. Her eyes were watering and she sputtered, but she went right back down on me, taking my entire length once again.

My balls tightened, and I knew my orgasm was moments away. I yanked myself out of her mouth and pointed my cock at her pretty tits, releasing my cum all over them.

As I did, she began to shake lightly. She reached for Gus's head and pulled him tighter into her pussy. "Oh god, yes, like that, god, I'm gonna come," she screamed and writhed as an orgasm hit her.

Gus pulled back after a moment and looked at her, spread for the world to see. "Such a pretty pussy. Jake, you want some now?" he asked.

Of course I did.

Not surprisingly, it was only a few minutes before I found myself hard again. I sat back on the sofa where Nella had been, and pulled her on top of me. She dangled her delicious tits in my face while I pried her open, still wet and swollen with need from Gus's ministrations.

"How're you doing baby?" I asked. "You feeling okay? Your pussy's not sore, is it?"

She shook her head, whimpering, shifting her hips to rub my cock.

But I kept moving it around on her. I wanted to make sure she was truly ready for a good fucking, and that she knew what was coming.

"You sure you can take me?" I whispered in her ear, spraying little kisses on her neck and occasionally tweaking her hard nipples.

"I'm sure, Jake," she panted, reaching between us to rub her clit.

Poor thing, she was so desperate for relief. It would have been unkind not to help her.

I looked over her shoulder at Gus, who'd

propped his ass on the edge of the desk, and who was slowly stroking himself, smiling happily as he stared at Nella's back view.

I held out my hand toward Gus, who immediately knew what I wanted. He reached into his jeans pocket and retrieved a condom, which he tossed over to me.

After I'd sheathed myself, I took aim at Nella's soft pussy, waiting impatiently for me. I pushed the hand she was using to play with herself out of the way and placed my own thumb on her clit while holding my cock in my other hand.

As soon as I found her opening, she slipped down on me, slowly but steadily, until I was balls deep in her and she was only able to moan, her head hanging limply onto her chest.

"You good, darlin'?" I asked.

"Yeah," she breathed without opening her eyes. Then she rolled her head back. "So fucking good, Jake."

Moving my hands to her hips, I rode her up and down my dick until her walls gripped me just like they had a couple nights before. With a rush of wetness, she convulsed and screamed, shuddering as she came all over my dick.

"Fuck me," I heard Gus mumble from a few feet away.

I could imagine his view of Nella from behind, watching her ride my dick, all wet and swollen with need, and then seeing her entire body tense as she contracted around me, milking me until I felt my own orgasm rising.

I reached up to her head and tangled my fingers in her black hair until I held fistfuls of it, and using that for leverage, pulled her down until I was buried balls deep inside her. Everything on my body tightened for a moment, and then with the slightest mix of pleasure and pain, I shot my load, surrounded by the vibrating walls of her pussy.

Gus must have realized how spent the two of us were, because he came over and lifted her off me. He gestured for me to lay down on the sofa, and he placed her next to me. I threw an arm over her and he flicked out the light, and shut the door quietly behind himself.

28

NELLA BRYSON

HAD SOMEONE GOTTEN TO THE GARAGE BEFORE ME?

I was usually the first to arrive. Not that I was Miss Punctual or anything. It's just that I was an early riser. It was one of my super powers. Need a ride to the airport at an ungodly hour?

I'm your girl.

I'd be late for everything else. But not something early in the morning.

Gus hadn't moved into the garage yet and Sebastian never arrived until the last possible moment, always having gotten his coffee first. That left Jake.

And my suspicion was confirmed when, of all people, his sister Louise stormed out the door, heading straight toward me until she finally looked up.

I didn't know whether to say hello or slug her.

I decided to start slowly. "Louise. What are you doing here at the garage? How did you get in?"

She put her hands on her hips and pressed her lips together so hard I don't know how her face didn't crack. "Morning," she hissed. "I... I came to talk to my brother."

"Is everything okay, Louise? What's going on?"

"Nothing. Don't worry about it," she huffed, and ran to her car.

Nothing my ass. That woman was pure trouble and I didn't like her being anywhere nearby. Who knew what the hell she was up to.

"Jake?" I asked, running into the shop. "Jake?"

I poked my head into the locker room, where I found him standing, one arm against the wall, looking like he wanted to punch something with the other.

"I saw your sister leaving. Is everything okay?"

He scraped his fingers through his hair and took a deep breath. "She's at it again."

"What? What does that mean?"

He took my hand and led me to the office. We sat

in the same spot where we'd messed around the evening before.

Goddamn if that wasn't hot...

Focus, you idiot.

"Jake, please tell me what's going on. I'm getting worried," I pleaded.

He leaned his head back on the sofa before he looked at me. "She knows you've messed around with all three of us guys. She said you're a... slut, and that if we don't call it off, she's going to make sure your father knows."

Oh my god.

The loathsome woman was a hideous excuse for a human being. There was just no other way to describe her.

This was far worse than what she'd done when I was in high school. By telling my father that I'd been intimate with all the guys, she might hurt me but especially them, putting their jobs at risk.

I wasn't sure how Dad would react, but I couldn't imagine he'd be too pleased that all his employees had been with his daughter. He couldn't really fire me, but he sure as hell could give the guys the heave-ho. Even if it hurt his business until he got new mechanics in the shop.

"I'm sorry, Nella. I'm so sorry."

I turned to him. "Jake, it's not your fault. Not

now, and not back when we were in high school. She's just a… sad little person."

"Initially I thought she was bluffing, blowing hot air to get me riled up. You know how she is. I told her we were all consenting adults and it was nobody's business what we did."

I covered my eyes with a hand as a wave of dizziness came over me.

"That's when she doubled down and screamed she'd tell everyone we were having orgies here at the shop. She's crazy."

"How does she know any of this?"

"I suspect she's been spying. Sniffing around the shop without our knowledge. I think she heard you'd come back to town and… well, you know. I'm so sorry."

He buried his head in his hands. "I can't believe my own sister would do this."

The shop door opened and closed and I heard voices.

Sebastian and Gus had arrived and were checking on a car.

"I… I wasn't going to tell anyone. But since you ran into her, there was no avoiding it. And if you can believe it, when she finished her diatribe, she actually asked me to fix her car."

That made me laugh. At least there was something funny to come out of this mess.

"What did you tell her?" I asked.

He exhaled a little gust of air. "I told her to take a hike, of course. If her car broke down in the middle of the freeway right now, I'd be hard pressed to help her."

"I'm sorry, Jake. I'm sorry she's doing this to you."

He took my hands. "No, I'm the one who is sorry. She's *my* family. If anything goes wrong here, it will be my fault. And your father has been so good to me…. " His voice trailed off.

"Just before she left, she screamed how I thought I was so much better than her."

Poor Jake. He looked exhausted. And sad. I just wanted to wrap my arms around him but I had another priority at the moment.

Bryson's Garage. I was supposed to be running it, keeping it afloat. Dad had entrusted his life's work to me

"Why'd she say that?" I asked.

Jake shook his head. "I guess because I've been getting ready for college, that means I'm better than her."

In spite of my long-lived resentment against Jake, I'd always thought his situation was… unfortunate. His family never had the money to send him to college, so he'd just assumed he never would. It was damn impressive that all these years later it was finally a possibility.

"Why so glum?" Gus asked, as he and Sebastian piled into my office.

Jake waved the question away. "Family drama. That's all."

I was willing to follow his lead on keeping the sordid tale to ourselves.

"Here's everybody's coffee," Sebastian said, setting them out on my desk. "And yes, I put one sugar in yours, Nella."

I laughed. Thank you."

He clapped his hands together and everyone looked his way. "So. Since we're all gathered here and the customers haven't started streaming in yet, I thought I'd bring up something we guys had wanted to discuss with you, Nella."

I looked around.

Were they all quitting?

Or asking for raises?

Or something else?

"Um, okay," I said, taking a tiny sip of my steaming coffee.

"We… we all like you, Nella," he said.

Oh, how sweet.

I smiled at them. "Thank you. I like you guys too."

The room went dead silent.

Was that it? Was that all they wanted to discuss?

I reached for a stack of papers on my desk and started fiddling. Something was going on. And I really didn't need any more drama for one morning.

"Guys. If you have something on your mind, please just tell me," I said, trying to sound cheery.

But dreading whatever new shit was coming my way.

"I don't think you understand, Nella. We *like* you. As in, want to date you," he continued.

I coughed a little, having choked on my coffee. "Oh. Um. Wow."

Date three guys? Yeah, right. I don't think they even did shit like that in New York.

Did they?

"I'm... I'm not sure how something like that would work."

Gus laughed. "Well, we're not exactly experts, either. But we'd like to give it a try."

Jake smiled, the upset of earlier having been momentarily forgotten. "That is, if you are on board. Only if you are on board."

"Darlin', you don't have to answer us now. Just think about it. In fact," he said, looking at the other guys, "I suggest we all have dinner together tonight and discuss it further," Gus said.

Well, that could work...

"Let's hit the steak place in the next town over. I've heard good things about it," he added.

I nodded slowly. "I like it. That's a great idea, to get together away from the shop."

"It's a date, then," Jake said, following the guys out of the office to get down to work.

I WAS nervous but also kind of excited for dinner. It really did feel like a date.

And god knew I hadn't been on one of those in a gazillion years.

There were lots of guys in Manhattan for sure, but I'd been going through the dry spell from hell.

Well, except for the weird guys who came into Mug Me on occasion, leaving notes on their tables.

Call me. I have a big dick.

Stuff like that. Classy. Romantic. Just what every girl wants.

My friend Jelly and I hung those on the wall of the employee bathroom for laughs.

I pulled on some black tights and a short skirt—and then took them right off.

My New York uniform of all or nearly all black was a bit too funereal for small town USA. So, I pulled on a pair of blue jeans and dove into my mom's closet.

I didn't have much hope there'd be anything in there that didn't look totally dated, but when I found a plain, white cotton blouse, I was psyched.

Pulling it on, I got a very faint whiff of her perfume.

Shit. Was this a mistake? I plopped down on my parents' bed and looked around the room, letting the tears come.

I didn't know how Dad did it, surrounded by her things day in and day out, like the house was some sort of memorial. But it worked for him, and I'd never want to take that away.

I rolled up the too-long sleeves and tied a little knot at my waist. Then, I spotted Mom's jewelry box.

She wasn't a fancy person, and I knew she didn't have anything of great value, but I lifted the lid anyway, in case there was something inspiring.

And I found her wedding band.

I rolled the simple white gold ring around in my fingers. I hadn't seen it in so many years, I'd forgotten about it. Dad probably had, too. I unclasped the silver chain around my neck, and slipped the ring onto it. Swiping on my signature red lipstick, I took a look in the mirror and heard the words of my mom, which I hadn't even thought of in so many years.

Nella, you are just like your father. Strong, capable, and stubborn. You can handle anything that comes your way.

Remembering her words left me shaking. I'd been lucky to have had her. All these years I'd focused on how she'd been taken from us. But maybe I should have looked at how lucky I was to have had her as long as I did.

My phone buzzed with a text from Jake, ripping me out of my reverie.

out front. come on down.

I looked in the mirror one last time. I looked okay. Good, even.

Thanks, Mom.

29

GUS MARTINS

"So what do you think?"

I paced the sidewalk in front of Bryson's Garage, but forced myself to stop. I didn't want to draw any attention, especially from Nella. She already had a shit-ton on her mind.

I took my cell phone off speaker and put it up to my ear. "I… I don't know. I'll tell you, Andy. It's real tempting to be hired outright, rather than go through the state program like I currently am. Don't get me wrong, my boss Bud has been good to me. But, thanks to the program, everybody around me knows my past."

I'd thought I was starting over when I'd arrived in town. But it seemed there was only so much of my past I could leave behind. Going to a new town altogether might help solve that.

"I can pay you more, Gus. I know you are talented as hell and a hard worker," he said.

Andy, my friend from the 'before days' as I called them, was a good guy. We'd both tinkered with cars when we were growing up, and now he'd opened his own shop.

I was the first person he thought of.

Which felt damn good.

Yeah. It was good to be wanted. Actually, it was fucking great. I'd been treated like a pariah by so many people for so damn long I'd forgotten what it felt like.

And last night's dinner with Nella and the guys hadn't exactly made me want to stick around.

It had been a nice evening until Jake's sister interrupted us.

How she even knew we were there was beyond me. Seriously. Was she some sort of fucking spy?

A nutcase spy, as the case may be.

"Well, look who's out to dinner tonight," she'd said, suddenly appearing at our table.

I, apparently, was the only one who didn't know who she was because Jake turned dead white, Nella choked on her wine, and Sebastian laughed loudly enough to turn heads.

Those were some damn strong reactions.

The woman looked around the table like she was deciding which of us she wanted to eat. And when she got to me, she looked me up and down, wandering closer.

"I'm Louise," she said, extending her hand. "Louise *Parker*." She glanced at her brother, then back to me with a smile.

"Oh. No shit. You're related to Jake?"

She nodded slowly.

I could tell from the rest of the table that this was not exactly a good thing.

"What do you want, Louise?" Nella said stiffly.

Louise's eyebrows rose, and she clicked her tongue. "Nothing, Nella. I was just having dinner over there with my friends, and wanted to come say hi. But it is especially nice to meet your new man, Gus."

She ran a hand over my shoulder, feeling my muscles, in a move entirely too familiar for the situation.

I shrugged her off. But she just turned to Sebastian and did the same damn thing.

"If you two, Gus and Sebastian, are free after dinner, I'd love to buy you a drink."

Sebastian smirked. "Why not just get a drink for everyone, Louise? Or would that be too nice for you?"

Her eyes flashed, but she ignored the insult. "Because, one, Jake's my brother, and two, Nella is fucking all of you anyway."

Nella's hand tightened around her wine glass, and for a moment I wondered if it was about to go airborne.

But Jake, noticing the same, placed a hand on her arm. Firmly.

"So, guys," she said, running a finger along the back of my neck. "You know where I'll be."

Nella started to get up from her chair but again, Jake restrained her.

"Oh, and Jake. Don't forget what we discussed. If you care about your friends. Or the garage."

And she left.

The table was silent for a moment.

"God. I'm so sorry," Jake said, hanging his head.

"Hey man. Not your fault," Sebastian said.

"What the hell was that all about?" I asked.

Jake sighed. "I haven't had the chance to tell you, Gus. My sister knows about the four of us. She wants us to put a stop to it or she'll tell Bud. And god knows who else."

Jesus. Nice lady.

"Why the hell does she care what we do?" I laughed.

But no one else did.

"Because she's mean and bitter and hates me," Nella said, finishing her wine.

We ate in silence for a while before I spoke up. I had so many questions.

"Do we take her seriously? And do we care if she tells Bud or anyone else in town?"

Nella shook her head. "That won't work. My dad would flip. It would be a mess."

"Really? Bud seems like such a cool guy—"

But the look Nella shot me said to drop it.

"Guys. There's no way what you propose would work." She lowered her voice. "You know, that we all date."

More silence.

"If that's the way you feel, Nella, we respect that," Sebastian said, rubbing the back of his neck.

Huh?

Now it was time for me to set my fork down. "Okay, everyone. Let's hold on. We're going to let that lunatic—sorry Jake—dictate how we live our lives?"

I knew the answer when we all looked at Nella.

If she wasn't in, then shit was all over.

So, my friend Andy's offer to come work for him was looking better and better. Much as I liked Bryson's, if Nella wasn't going to be part of my life in the way I hoped she would, sticking around had just become a lot less attractive.

GUS MARTINS

I SLIPPED INTO A BOOTH AT THE LOCAL DINER AND checked my watch.

Fifteen minutes.

I was always early for meetings with my parole officer. If there was one thing they taught me as I was leaving prison, it was that my parole officer was my new best friend.

I also learned that if there was anybody who could get your ass back to prison in the blink of an eye, it was them. You practically couldn't take a shit without first getting permission.

"Gus. You're looking well," Pete said, sliding into the booth opposite me.

He flipped open a notebook with tiny writing—too small for me to read upside down—and paused his pen on the page while looking back at me, smiling.

"Thanks, Pete. You look well, too. Good to see you."

"You too. So hey, I understand things at Bryson's Garage are going well. That's great news."

"Yeah, they really are. I feel lucky. But I'm curious. How did you manage to check on things at the garage?"

"I just spoke to…" he flipped through his notebook, "Nella. Nella Bryson. I take it she's the owner?"

I shook my head. "Owner's daughter."

Nodding, Pete leaned closer after the waitress served him his coffee.

"Hey, Gus, by any chance… you two have something going on?"

His out of line question left me chafing. But I could remain cool.

"Wow, Pete," I said, looking out the diner window. "I didn't realize probation officers monitored, you know… our love lives."

Pete shrugged. "We usually don't. It was just a

vibe I got. Could be totally wrong. But look, if that's the case, I would just ask you to think hard about what you're doing. You're lucky to have this job and I wouldn't want any drama to threaten it. You're in a good place, Gus. Keep up the great work."

I felt a degree of calm wash over me, but that didn't make me any more diplomatic. "While I appreciate your concern, I am pretty sure this bit is really none of your business."

To his credit, Pete was unfazed. "You're probably right, Gus. I shouldn't even have brought it up. But one thing I can tell you is that you can't live at the garage."

Jesus, how did this fucker know every last detail about my life?

"All right. Can you tell me why?" I asked.

He sighed. "Part of your probation is showing you can live in traditional housing, paying your rent and utilities and such. You're not allowed to squat."

Fuck me. How was staying at the garage squatting?

But I kept my questions to myself. I was sure my frustration would come through in my voice and this was one person I needed to have a good relationship with.

"Understood, Pete. I'll correct the situation ASAP. The place I've been living, the landlady found out about my record *after* I moved in, and when she did, she flipped."

"Damn. I'm sorry that happened, Gus. But you know to keep moving forward. You have your shit together. You can handle anything life on the outside throws your way," he said. "This won't be the first challenge, and it won't be the last."

I knew he was right.

Just then my phone rang.

"Pete, can you hold on a sec? I'd like to take this call from Nella, the woman you spoke to."

He nodded and headed to the men's room.

"Hey, Nella, I'm meeting with my probation officer at the diner. What's up?"

I heard her office door close in the background.

"I know you're there. He came by just before heading over to you."

"Okay."

"He didn't seem to like that you were going to stay at the garage for a while."

I sighed. "You are absolutely right. He said that was a no-go. I had no idea. So, I guess I'm back to square one."

That offer from my friend Andy was looking more attractive with every passing minute.

Pete returned from the rest room and I gave him the 'one minute' signal.

"Gus, I was thinking," Nella said. "So you can't stay at the garage, fine. But I don't think there's any rule saying you can't stay at my dad's house."

Holy shit.

I cleared my throat to keep my cool. "Um. That's a generous offer. Let me discuss it with Pete here."

I wondered why she'd thrown that offer at me. I guess she was just being generous, and figured her father's house would be empty when she went back to New York, anyway. Either way, it was an awesome thing to do.

"What's up, Gus?" Pete asked when I'd swiped my phone closed.

I didn't want to get too excited. He'd probably shoot this idea down like he did the garage.

"That was Nella, as you know. She had an idea. One that could help with my living situation."

Pete nodded with interest. "Tell me."

"I'd have to give it some thought myself, but she said since living at the garage was a no-go, that I could rent a room in her father's house. She's staying there now, but will be heading back to New York eventually. I guess at some point, her father will be back in the house, so of course I want to make sure he's okay with it. But, it sounds promising."

Pete looked at me for a moment, considering.

And while I was surprised by Nella's offer, especially since she said that she couldn't possibly date us guys, I was hoping like hell that Pete wouldn't see anything wrong with this potential situation.

"You know…" he started to say, "I think this could be okay. I mean, if you're, you know, with Miss Bryson, I'd be careful, but as long as you can prove you're there legitimately and so forth, I think it would be fine."

Fuck yeah.

Those Brysons were good people, always taking care of me without fail. I hoped that I could someday pay it forward.

But until I could, I had plans to show Nella how grateful I was.

Very grateful.

31

NELLA BRYSON

"WHAT ARE YOU WEARING?"

My fingers flew to my neck, where I felt Mom's wedding band on the silver chain. I'd nearly forgotten it was there.

"Oh yeah. It's Mom's," I said casually, wondering if there was going to be an issue.

I braced myself for a lecture. I knew Dad wouldn't be happy about my using my mother's things, and I wanted to kick myself for not remembering to remove it before I'd popped in to visit.

He pressed his lips together while he stared. The memories must have been overwhelming.

When he didn't say anything for a while, I was compelled to fill the silence.

"I hope this doesn't upset you, Dad. I know how you are about her things."

Which meant I shouldn't have touched anything of hers, much less helped myself to it. I made a mental note to stuff the white blouse I'd worn deep into my bag so he didn't see it when he returned home. If I wasn't gone before he got there.

And yes, I planned to keep the blouse for myself. It wasn't doing him any good, was it?

He carefully scooted over in his bed, patting a spot for me to sit on.

When I'd settled in, keeping a foot on the floor so I didn't jostle him, he took one of my hands.

Okay this was weird. My dad had never taken my hand. I wasn't sure he even ever took my mother's hand.

"I'm okay with you wearing Mom's wedding band. It looks beautiful on you. I can't think of a better use for it."

Holy crap. Had he really just said that?

Because I freaking loved wearing it.

"You know, Nella, how I was in such pain for so long over losing your mother that I couldn't share anything of hers. It was like she was moving further and further away from me as time passed. I was afraid, more than anything, that I might forget her. Looking back, I know that was silly."

Oh god. Here come the tears.

Dad passed me a tissue from the little table next to his bed.

"I thought if I shared her, there'd be less for me."

I nodded, broken-hearted by Dad's admission.

I'd been fifteen or so when we lost Mom to cancer, and of course at that age I was a head-up-my-ass teenager and didn't much care about anyone but myself. Being so wrapped up in my own grief, I'd not paid any attention to my father's. All I knew was that I was not to touch Mom's stuff.

I'd never blamed him, though.

"I was an ass, Nella."

"No, Dad. No you were not. It was a hard time for all of us. If anyone was an ass, it was me."

He shook his head. "You were a teenager. You were supposed to be an ass. I was not."

I had to laugh at that one.

"Well, you did the best you could."

"Oh, sometimes I wonder. But you and your brother—look at you. Adults now, living on your own in the big city. I must have done something right."

I squeezed his hand back. "I think you did a lot of things right. The guys down at the garage adore you.

I mean, I think they'd follow you over a cliff if you asked them"

He dropped his head back and laughed. "Those assholes?"

"Very funny, Dad. Hey, speaking of the garage, how are you feeling? When are you coming back?"

Suddenly excited, he pushed himself up in bed. "Oh, good news. I'm doing really well and won't have to be here as long as we thought I might."

I felt something drop in my stomach.

What the hell was wrong with me? I should be jumping up and down. After all, hadn't I wanted to get the hell out of this place since the day I'd arrived?

Yeah. I'd been jonesing for New York on a daily basis. It was where I was meant to be.

It was just that I wasn't ready to go back… yet.

I mean, I would be, eventually. I guess.

What was the freaking hesitation? I had nothing keeping me here.

Or did I?

"So what's your timeframe, Dad? When are you expected home?" I asked, my voice cracking.

He waved away my question. "Oh. I'm not coming home."

I frowned at him. "Huh?"

"Well, I've wanted to talk to you about this. I've already told your brother."

Glad the jerk took Dad's calls. He sure didn't take mine.

"What did you tell Robbie? What do I need to know?"

"It's all very exciting. Dakini and I are going backpacking through Europe. Probably for a year or so. Maybe longer. We might include Asia. Check out some ashrams. Attend a yoga retreat or two. Practice silent meditation. We might even go vegan."

He was beaming. Positively beaming.

What the actual fuck?

"Um, Dad, you are recovering from a badly broken leg—"

He patted my hand. "Honey, I didn't say we were leaving *tomorrow*."

I jumped off his bed and started to pace. This was weird. And confusing.

I'd just been shredded by the thought that the time had come for me to leave the garage and head back to New York.

If I wasn't ready to leave, then why the hell was I pissed that Dad assumed I'd stay indefinitely so he could act like he didn't have a care in the world?

And where had he gotten the notion of freaking backpacking in freaking Europe? Sixty-year-old owners of car repair shops didn't do shit like that.

I took a breath to calm myself. I knew Dad would

never listen if I got shrill. After all, I'd inherited my stubbornness from the champ.

"Dad, you are not a twenty-year-old college student trying to find himself."

Neither was Dakini, but she wasn't my problem. And besides, she was probably closer to my age than Dad's.

And did she have any idea about the shows she was putting on for the neighborhood men?

I continued my diatribe. "You should be slowing down, Dad. Sailing into your sunset years. Playing cards with your buddies. Fishing. Stuff like that."

"To hell with that!" he exploded.

Shit. Now I'd done it.

"I'm tired of looking out for everyone but myself. I'm in love. Dakini and I are in love!" he shouted.

Oh god. I took a seat in the guest chair and looked around for a trash can in case I got sick.

He held up a finger like he did when I was a kid and had done something wrong. It was a wonder I wasn't shaking from head to toe.

"It's my time to enjoy life. The garage is your problem now. I built it up for you, and you can have it. You know how many people would love to be handed a thriving, successful business for free?"

No, I didn't know. But I was pretty sure I wasn't one of them.

"Dad, you can't do this. I don't… I don't want the business. I want to get back to New York."

Something about those words, getting back to New York, tasted *off*. Like milk just starting to sour.

He threw his hands up. "Fine. Sell the garage then. Just don't bother me about it anymore."

Wait. What. Had he really just said that?

"No. No freaking way, Dad—"

"You are not killing my dreams! Nobody is—"

"Mr. Bryson, is there a problem?" an annoyed-looking nurse asked. "You are disturbing people with your yelling."

He slammed his hand down on the bed. "Yes, there is a problem. It's my turn to be happy!" he shouted.

Her eyes grew wide, and she nodded slowly. Unsure what to do with Dad's outburst, she gradually backed out of the room.

Fuck. It was like listening to a bratty teenager.

It was like listening to myself, several years ago.

Dad had been saddled with responsibilities all his life. He'd never had the privilege of being a bratty teenager.

Could he be one now?

"Why are you slamming things around, Nella?" Jake asked, entering the office with the other guys. "What's wrong?"

I plopped down in my chair and put my head in my hands. "Dad just informed me he's not coming back to the garage. That it's mine. And when I told him I didn't want it, he said it wasn't his problem."

Sebastian wrinkled his brow. "He's not coming back? Where the hell is he going?"

To emphasize the absurdity of the situation, I jumped to my feet.

"He's going—get this, and try not to have a freaking heart attack—backpacking in Europe with his hot new girlfriend."

Indignant, I looked from one guy to the next, expecting all the sympathy, commiseration, and more, that I desired.

Instead, they glanced at each other sheepishly and shrugged.

"That sounds… fucking awesome," Gus said after a painful silence.

Sebastian and Jake agreed, nodding cautiously.

"What? *What?* Are you crazy?"

Jake shrugged one shoulder. "Why shouldn't he have his fun? Everybody else gets to."

Oh my god. I should have known the guys would side with him. Men always did shit like that.

"Fine. Whatever, guys. I have work to do." I turned back to the bank statements that had come in the mail, which I was trying, unsuccessfully, to understand.

The guys filed out, one by one, without a word. But I could see through the office window that once out of my hearing, they were talking animatedly, laughing, and slapping each other on the back.

Everybody was happy about the news except for me.

Was I missing something?

It didn't matter. I'd tell Sebastian to take over the garage. Gus could stay in the house. I was leaving town. Between Jake's crazy sister stalking me and trying to make trouble for us all, and the fact that I couldn't run a garage any more than I could run, well, anything, there was no place for me in this town.

Even though I had a built-in job, place to live, and friends like Izzy who would do anything for me.

And three hot men who adored me.

No, I had no reason to stick around.

None at all.

32

NELLA BRYSON

"When is he moving in?"

I looked up from my desk. "Who?"

"Gus. He said he's moving into your house. Well, your dad's house."

Oh. That.

"Not sure, Seb. I gave him keys and told him to have at it. It doesn't much matter, because I'm leaving soon anyway. We need to tell my dad you'll be running things from now on."

He rolled his eyes. "C'mon, Nella. Aren't we all in this together?"

He took several steps toward my desk, and in

spite of my shitty mood and self-pity party, I felt a clenching in my core.

Damn him. Dude was my childhood crush and all the years that had passed hadn't done much to put out that fire.

He plopped into the chair opposite me, smelling slightly of motor oil and a little perspiration mixed with simple, clean soap. And I'd never smelled anything sexier.

I was so fucked.

"I can't do it Seb," I said, my voice catching.

Ugh. I didn't want to cry in front of this guy. Or anyone.

He leaned his elbows on my desk, and a lock of crazy messy hair fell across his forehead.

I so wanted to smooth that off his face…

"Nell, don't worry about the townies. Who cares what they think or say? Shit, if you knew half the stuff that went down in this town, your head would spin. You may be here from the big city, but folks here have some quirks that would put New York to shame."

"Really?"

Wait. We weren't sitting here to talk about the other people in town. We had our own shit to resolve.

And that was making sure that Sebastian knew

that the guys and I were not a 'thing,' nor would we ever be.

But damn if he wasn't weakening my resolve.

While he talked, my gaze was glued to his full lips, remembering how he ran them over my…

Easy girl.

"Nella, we've got to give this a try. Look, my lease is almost up and you know Jake lives in that shithole over the laundromat. We've been talking about getting a place together. We can all move into your place and see how things work out. It's the only way we'll know."

There was a knock on my office door, and Jake joined us.

"I was just telling Nell about our idea," Sebastian said.

Jake's eyebrows rose. "And?"

I shook my head. "The answer's no. We can't. For one, consider my brother. What the hell would he think?"

Jake and Sebastian looked at each other.

"When was the last time Robbie thought of you?"

They had a point.

I placed my hands flat on my desk. I wanted to be very clear. "Look, Seb, I know there's some bad blood between you and my brother—" I started to say.

He frowned, interrupting me. "But there's not. There's no bad blood. Our lives have gone in different directions. That's all. It happens. I'm not saying forget about Robbie with any sort of malicious or bitter intention. He's just... not that interested in what we do here. And that's fine."

I hadn't thought of it that way. I'd taken personally the regular insults my brother flung my way. But in truth, he was like that to everyone.

It was his loss for passing up a friendship with someone as awesome as Sebastian.

"Nell. I'm focusing on happy. And you are my happy. And while I can't speak for the other guys, I'd bet they are thinking the same," Sebastian said, looking at Jake.

Well shit. And now the lump in my throat was growing.

He wasn't done. "You know how long it took me to get to where I am in my life? A lot of shit went down with my family, and what a relief it was when my mom finally left my dad. *Your* father gets all the credit for making me the man I am today. No one else would ever have given me the boost he did."

"Same here," Jake said.

Gus stuck his head in the office. "Me, too."

"If you stay, Nella," Sebastian said, "you'll be

giving me—and Jake and Gus—the one thing we don't have in our lives."

"He's right," Gus said. "You know my friend offered me a job downstate. But I have everything I need here. Except for one thing. And I ain't giving up on that."

These guys were good. Really good.

"Tell me, Nella," Jake said, "don't you wonder, at least a little bit, whether the four of us could make it work?"

Dammit. A headache was now circling my head like a vulture looking for a place to land. I was done. Just done.

I grabbed my bag. "Sorry, guys. I'm not feeling well. I'll check in later."

And I ran out to my car, leaving behind the three most amazing men I'd ever known.

IZZY MADE some weird little motion with her fingers. "You know what this is?"

I watched her for a moment. "No. No, I don't."

She put her hands closer to my face. "This is the world's tiniest violin. I'm playing the world's saddest song for you, the girl who has a nice house, a ready-made business, and three hot guys who adore her.

Must be terrible. Awful. I don't know what I'd do if I were in your shoes."

I gave her my best stink-eye. But she kept up her violin game.

"Are there any song requests before you throw yourself in front of a train?" she taunted. "Only sad songs allowed. Tragic ones are even better."

So. Funny.

"I can't do it, Izz. This town already thinks I'm a freak for leaving and going to New York.

She shrugged, rubbing her huge belly. "Then, do what I do."

I frowned. "What's that?"

She signed with impatience. "Do you think every person in this town loves me? I mean, I *am* loveable, no question about it," she cackled, "but there are some crazy idiots out there who are not fans. And you know what?"

"What?"

"Fuck them."

Right. Easy for her to say.

"Who cares what other people think?" she added. "I don't."

"But... but I do care... what other people think," I stammered.

"And why is that?" Izzy asked.

I had to think about that for a moment. "I... I don't know. I just do."

She lay her hands on the diner counter, just next to my double chocolate milk. "Are you happy, Nell?"

I nodded, trying to convince myself as much as anyone. "Yeah. Yes."

Izzy tipped her head. "Are you happy with the guys?"

"Yeah. They're great. But why—"

She held her hand up to stop me. "Stop. No buts. You know what you have to do. Go do it."

I considered what she said for so long I thought she might throw me out for not having any guts. She wandered off to serve coffee to a bunch of new customers, and then returned.

She didn't say a word. Just raised an eyebrow.

"You... you are right, Izz. To hell with everyone else," I said, not really sure of my words but liking the way they felt in my mouth.

She slammed her hand on the countertop so hard everyone in the diner turned to see what was going on.

With our gazes locked, I stood from the counter, trying to think through my next move.

And as I did, Izzy shooed me out with two hands. "Go get your guys, Nell."

BEFORE I MADE my next move, there was something I needed to get off my chest. I drove to Jake's parents' house where his sister, Louise, still lived.

She came to the door right away and when she saw it was me, her eyes widened. But after registering surprise, she went right back to her tough girl act.

"Yeah?" she asked with a contemptuous sniff. "You here to tell me off? Maybe punch me in the nose?"

Shaking her head, she looked up and laughed. It was as if she'd been waiting for me.

And instead of feeling anger, I was just curious. And a little sad for her.

"Louise. I don't want to do any of those things."

She came out on the front porch and faced me with crossed arms.

"I want to know what your beef is with me."

She looked down, then up, then at the horizon. Anywhere but at me.

And shrugged.

"You don't know?"

She shook her head. "You… you always get what you want. You always have."

I was speechless, so I just stared at her. The years

hadn't been kind and even though she was just a few years older than Jake and me, time had taken its toll, leaving her with an unhealthy, gray complexion, and the start of some very deep lines around her lips.

And she looked tired. Really tired.

"Me? How do I get everything I want? Don't you remember how I lost my mom when I was fifteen? You think that wasn't horrible? It upended my life. I've never been the same. I kept moving forward, yeah, because if I didn't, I wasn't sure I would survive."

"You've had such a great life," she said quietly.

"So that's a reason to fuck with me? Like it will make your life better to mess up someone else's? And I know what you did in high school, spreading rumors. I know everything now."

She looked down at her feet. "I don't know what's wrong with me," she said quietly.

"Louise, I love your brother."

The words came tumbling out so fast, I wasn't sure which of us was more surprised.

She sniffled and looked at me. "What are you gonna do?"

"I... I'm still figuring that out. I'll have to let you know."

⚒

33

JAKE PARKER

"Is something burning?"

I walked into Nella's kitchen and saw a pan with charred steaks, still sizzling in their juices, smoking enough that Sebastian was running to open all the windows as well as the door leading to the backyard.

"Something *was* burning, but it's not now. Gus and I got here just in time to make sure the Bryson family house would be standing for another few decades instead of being reduced to ashes."

Nella, wearing a hilarious apron that must have once been her mother's, sheepishly dumped the steaks into the kitchen garbage can and tossed the ruined pan after it.

"At least the sweet potatoes and other side dishes came out okay."

I looked around. "Where is Gus, by the way?"

"He ran to the store for more steaks. He'll be right back. In the meantime, how about a beer?" Sebastian offered, diving into the fridge.

I accepted one and took a seat at the kitchen counter. Damn, it had been a long time since I'd been in the Bryson's house. I'd spent a lot of time there, back in the day.

But not as much time as Sebastian. He'd practically been raised by the Brysons.

"So Nell, your Betty Crocker skills are not quite ready for prime time then?"

Sebastian laughed. Hard.

She threw him a stink eye. "Well. I don't cook a lot in New York. My roommates kind of bogart the kitchen when they're not fucking each other, so I stick to cereal or take out. Guess I'm kind of rusty."

"Or a pyromaniac," Sebastian laughed.

The front door opened and slammed, and a breathless Gus rushed in.

"Hey, kids, I'm back for round two. This time, I'm taking over," he said.

Nella rolled her eyes after a swig of beer. "Whatever. Here. You must wear my mother's apron."

She lifted it over her head, and lowered it over Gus's. When he straightened back up, we nearly all fell over.

Here was a giant of a man, wearing something intended for a small woman. The sides of the apron were up to his armpits, and the straps, which Nella tried to tie behind his back, weren't long enough to reach.

"That's fucking hot, dude," I said. "You are seriously going to rake in the babes."

He looked down at himself. "I can just imagine the guys back at prison seeing me dressed like this. It wouldn't be pretty."

Nella went to lift the apron back over his head, having sufficiently hazed him. But he stopped her.

"No, no. Don't take my apron away. I'm wearing this baby. I'm committed. Now, let's head to the grill so we can do these juicy steaks some justice."

Sebastian fired Bud's old grill up and Gus set to work making us a second dinner since Nella had bungled the first attempt.

We sat around the picnic table while Gus hilariously cooked in his apron, sipping our beers, and admiring the warm evening.

We were not at all certain why Nella had invited

us over for dinner. She'd never done that before. But I, for one, was pretty sure it was to say goodbye or some such. It was clear to me she wasn't sticking around to either run her dad's business or be with us guys, and she was ready to hit the road back to New York.

But it was all good. We were grown men and we'd be fine.

Since it was nice enough to eat outdoors, we helped Nella move the entire dinner to the picnic table, and dove into the steaks, which Gus had prepared to perfection.

"I don't imagine you ate like this in prison, did you?" I asked.

"Oh hell no. But before I went in, I used to cook a lot. And I've always loved a good steak."

I took a bite of mine, and almost moaned, that's how perfect it was. In fact, the entire table was quiet for a good several minutes, enjoying the first home-cooked meal any of us had had in a while.

After I got back from fetching another round of beers from the fridge, Nella tapped her fork on her can and stood up.

"Well look at that. I think someone is about to make a speech," Sebastian said, looking at Nella with hungry eyes.

Actually, we were all looking at her with hunger,

and it wasn't the kind that was satisfied by a nice steak dinner.

But I think we'd also resigned ourselves to the fact that our attraction to Nella was going no further than it had. As much as we each hoped she'd stick around, work with us, and even be involved with us—whatever that exactly meant—we'd resolved ourselves to accepting that was just not going to happen.

At least that's what we thought at the time.

So, when Nella got to her feet, I know I was expecting some kind of goodbye speech. I wasn't happy about it, but I was resigned. What else could I do? If the woman had her mind set on getting back to New York, I knew better than to stand in her way.

"Jake, Sebastian, and Gus, thank you for coming to dinner tonight. And special thanks to Gus for *saving* the actual dinner."

He bowed his head modestly.

"Seriously, Gus," Sebastian said, "if you hadn't come through, we'd all be chowing down at McDonald's now."

Nella shot him a play stink-eye and continued. "What I wanted to say tonight is pretty simple, really."

She was so beautiful, standing in front of the three of us, speaking with a confidence I knew she'd earned only through her years away from our small town, where she had to find her own way in a strange city where she knew no one except her brother—and I wasn't sure he really even counted.

I looked around the Bryson home backyard, wondering if I'd ever be back there. With Nella leaving, and Bud sticking to his travel plans, I imagined the house would be sold and I'd never see the interior of it again.

I supposed that meant I'd never see Nella again, either.

And that hit like a hard lump of something indigestible in my gut. Shit did not feel good.

"If everyone is done with their smart-assed remarks about my cooking abilities, or lack of them, I have something important to say. First, I want to thank you for being so loyal to my father. I know he's a generous, good man, and I appreciate your recognizing and paying that forward. Next, I want to thank you for helping me slip into his role as best I could, and for being patient while I came up to speed on how he was running things. Turned out they weren't that different than they were when I was helping him with inventory ten years ago."

Everyone nodded and laughed.

Gus raised his beer. "Cheers to Bud Bryson. One of the most kick-ass men I've ever known."

A chorus of *cheers* went around, and Nella looked so proud I thought she might start to cry. Instead, she continued with her little speech.

"Last, I want to thank you for inviting me into your hearts. I don't know what I did to deserve the three of you—or even if I do deserve you—but I am so honored to be valued as I am by you. So, after a lot of thinking, I wanted to say… let's do it."

The table was silent for a moment while we waited for her to continue, and when she didn't, I asked for clarification.

"Do what, Nella? What are we doing?"

"Yeah, what are you saying, Nella?" Sebastian asked.

She took a deep breath. "My dad has given me everything. It took me a moment to realize how generous that was, and how lucky I am. And that I'd be an idiot to walk away. Not only from this great house, a successful business, a town where I have friends who for some reason put up with me through all my bullshit drama, and especially you. You guys. I feel kind of like in addition to everything else, he gave me the three of you."

Okay. This, I was not expecting. And from the looks of the other two guys, neither were they.

We pretty much just all sat there with our mouths hanging open.

Here I was ready to say goodbye to the only woman I'd ever loved, and now that was all turned on its head.

She wasn't saying goodbye?

She wasn't heading back to New York?

She wasn't passing up the opportunity to be with us?

Fuck yeah.

Sebastian ran his hand through his mop of hair, his brow furrowed. "So… you're saying we should stay together? Did I hear that right? I just want to make sure I really understand what's going on here."

But Gus seemed to have gotten it, because he jumped to his feet and ran over to Nella. He picked her up and twirled her until she screamed for mercy, laughing the whole time.

Dizzy from Gus's manhandling, she stumbled and caught her breath, grabbing the edge of the table for balance. "Yes, I am saying we should be together. You guys… well, I don't know why it took me so long to realize it… but I love you. There, I said it. If you don't feel it back, that's okay. Because I really believe that in time, you will love me. Just like I love you."

Now, it was my turn to jump to my feet. "Holy shit, Nell. This is incredible." I lay a big, juicy kiss on her lips, and grabbed a handful of her ass for good measure.

That left Sebastian to respond to the news. But he still just sat there, looking confused. So Nella took the wheel.

"Seb, honey," she said flirtatiously, hooking a finger under his chin, "tell me you're in. Tell me I didn't wait too long."

He looked up at her in disbelief. "Are you fucking kidding? There's no such thing. I mean, I would have sat around on my ass for the rest of my life waiting for you to come to your damn senses and realize you need to be with the three of us."

She broke into a huge grin, and threw her arms around him.

Gus and I were busy with high-fives while Nella ran into the house for an old bottle of champagne her dad had stashed in the back of the fridge. It might be a crappy bottle not worthy of our celebration, but it didn't matter. We had plenty of days—and nights—ahead to celebrate our good fortune, and while none of us knew what those times would look like, I was sure we'd find a way to enjoy them with laughter and lots of sexy, naked times.

EPILOGUE

Dear Nella Bella,
Greetings from Corfu. After weeks of museums
and cathedrals in every damn European city
(thanks to Dakini), we are now cruising the Greek
islands (thanks to me), starting with Corfu. Or as
they call it here, Kerkyra. You should see the place.
Brilliant, clear blue water, rocky beaches, old
monasteries. Great discos with parties that last all
night...

My dad was cruising? The Greek islands? Going to discos? Partying all night long?

The universe had somehow switched our lives.

While Dad was out in the world, 'finding himself,' I was running the show at home, at Bryson's Garage.

Which by the way, had a new 'y' in the sign. Only ten-plus years overdue.

But I had Jake, Sebastian, and Gus.

I was pretty sure I'd gotten the better deal.

My BFF Izzy had given birth to another girl. I'd been there to witness the whole crazy thing. Yup, they'd invited me. Turned out Izzy liked to have an audience. And this new girl—I was going to be her godmother.

My brother, Robbie, had started calling me on a

regular basis. Not because he gave a crap about me or the garage, or even what Dad was doing gallivanting with his hot young girlfriend, but because it turned out his lovely admin, Charlotte, and he had a thing. And she'd gotten knocked up.

That's right. Robbie had knocked up his admin, and they were thrilled.

Lucky for Robbie, it turned out having a sister like me could help navigate the world of relationships. So far, I'd kept him out of deep shit with my recommendations for buying nice gifts like pretty lingerie and chocolate, and, most importantly, keeping his big mansplaining mouth shut and listening when she talked to him. It seemed to be working. And miracle of miracles, Charlotte had actually started being nice to me on the phone when I called.

If she hadn't, well, that would make for some pretty awkward family holidays.

Louise Parker, Jake's sister from hell, seemed to be turning over a new leaf. But it wasn't completely by accident. Jake had taken the money he'd saved for college and split it between the two of them so they could both attend part-time. I was blown away by his generosity and loyalty toward someone who hadn't been all that nice to him. I was also kind of sad he wasn't realizing his dream quite the way he'd imagined it, of being a full-time student. But I had to admit I was happy to still have him around the garage, even if it was just part-time while he attended classes.

With Jake part-time, that meant more work for Gus and Sebastian, but they didn't complain. What they did gripe about, however, was my cooking. Since we were all living under one roof now, I thought I'd show off my skills and put dinner on the table every now and then. But the guys had pretty much banished me from the kitchen, with Gus taking the lead on our evening meals.

He was doing a seriously bang-up job.

And if I kept eating his cooking, I would soon need to get myself some new blue jeans.

Speaking of living arrangements, what I thought would be the biggest obstacle to committing to all the guys would be my dad. I mean, what father wants to see his daughter with three men. Who also happen to work for him?

Turned out no father wanted to see that.

Except my dad.

"My mechanics are some of the most righteous men I've ever known. I'm honored they want to be with my daughter," he'd said, nearly giving me a heart attack with his new-age openness.

Righteous was not a word I'd ever heard my father use.

But Dakini had introduced all sorts of new things to him.

When I thought about it, I realized I had her to thank for a lot of things too, most importantly, making my father a very, very happy man.

And when I thought about it further, I had her to thank for my new life, too. If Dad hadn't been spying on her, he wouldn't have fallen off the ladder. If Dad hadn't fallen off the ladder, I never would have left New York. If I'd never left New York, I never would have come back to run the garage.

Or have fallen in love with my sexy mechanics, Jake, Sebastian, and Gus.

Namaste.

Did you like *Her Dirty Mechanics*? Learn about the next book in the Men at Work series, *Her Dirty Detectives*

I hope you loved reading this book as much as I loved writing it. Please visit my store to learn more about my books, and to buy directly from me!

https://mikalaneshop.com/

SHOP
Mika
Lane

ABOUT THE AUTHOR

Dear Reader:

I'm USA TODAY bestselling romance author Mika Lane, and am OBSESSED with bringing you sassy, steamy stories with imperfect heroines and the bad-a*s dudes they bring to their knees. I'll always bring you my signature humor and heat, topped off with a modern-day happily ever after.

My first book ever was *The Day I Ate the Milkyway*, a true fourth-grade masterpiece illustrated with crayons and bound with construction paper and glue. Nowadays, steamy romance gives purpose to my days and nights as I create worlds and characters that tickle the imagination. I live in magical Northern California with my own handsome alpha dude, sometimes known as Mr. Mika Lane, and two devilish cats named Chuck and Murray.

A dual citizen of the United States and Ireland, I have on more than one occasion spent my last dollar on a plane ticket somewhere, and am always planning my next escape. I often try new recipes on unsuspecting friends, search out hiding places to read undisturbed, and sadly kill every houseplant I bring home.

I LOVE to hear from readers when I'm not dreaming up naughty tales to share. Visit my online shop https://mikalaneshop.com/ and say hello https://mikalaneshop.com/pages/meet-mika.

xoxo, Mika